www.united-pc.eu

MASTIFF AFV

A TANK CREWMANS TOUR OF

AFGHANISTAN

WRITTEN BY TROOPER MCCARTAN 1ST ROYAL
TANK REGIMENT

FORWARD

The account is written from dairies and journals which I wrote in when I was over in Afghanistan. I have added reports from media outlets concerning events to add authenticity to the accounts from my journals. The details of the different weapon systems are taken from my training journals and notes from pre-deployment. I think it is essential information as people do not understand the threats that are faced daily in theatre. The photos were taken on an IPOD either by myself or by a gunner or commander from the turret of the Mastiff. I can be contacted on @mastiffafv.

CONTENTS

PROLOGUE

21/03/2012 DAY ONE

.... Whoosh, whoosh, whoosh, the Mercian's dragged me into the back of the Mastiff, locked the doors and hatch, There was a succession of 3 explosions, one 25 yards away from our vehicle. The IDF alarm was blaring and people were running for hard cover all over the place. When IDF hits the drill is to lie down on your belly, hands over your eyes, and mouth open, or find hard cover. The shrapnel the shell makes when it hits the ground explodes in a funnel shape, so will hit you at height. The insurgents had used the cover of the sand storm to dig themselves in to different positions around the FOB. One of the LECs (locally employed civilians), had obviously tipped them off, that there was mass movement on camp, and it would be a good time to fire.

A 2 Mercian's Captain came over to get a section of lads together to go out on a quick foot patrol, to find the firing points. The lads that were with me, stayed to help with the handover. I carried on and signed for the wagon. My kit insurance would have easily hit the roof, if they were aware that a Trooper was signing for what could easily be £500,000 worth of kit, a used Mastiff 2 much cost a fortune, the signals kit, 2 GPMGs, the tools and the ECM, I wasn't comfortable doing it. Wee Des the only Gunner that got dicked to come up, and didn't bother helping came and got me for lunch, it was around 1130.

Mr McCullough met us and we queued for scoff. The lunch room was packed and it was hard to get a seat. We had only just sat down and a loud explosion shook the entire camp, you could feel the vibration in your body. Everyone thought it was more IDF and the place went mental. Hard cover was right next to the cookhouse and we dived in there. This was our first day on the ground and it was not yet 1200. I was stunned and then I heard someone speaking in derogatory terms about the Irish Rugby team. I turned around and my best mate from phase 1 training was there Thomas Warner, and why a Welsh man was discussing rugby I will never know. He was leaving the same day that I had arrived. He was living in the desert doing reconnaissance on CVRTs for the brigade with the QDGs, he couldn't get out due to the flight restrictions. It was good to see him.

News started to filter through that the explosion wasn't IDF, it was an IED and that a casualty was being brought in. An order came through for all non-essential personnel to stay away from the med centre which was next to where I had signed for my vehicle. A 2 Mercian Officer, Captain Rupert William Michael Bowers had stood on an Old Italian anti-personnel mine which must have been planted next to the base with the sandstorm for cover. Captain Bowers was in the middle of the section which is unusual as it's normally the first man that gets hit.

This was Captain Bowers final patrol before leaving theatre. He was only 24. Molly and Suthers seen him come back in, everything from below the chest was missing. As the casualty evacuation helicopter came into extract Captain Bowers, 3 more whooshes but slower than the first salvo. The insurgents had waited for the angel's flight and aimed at the Pedro. They had used a system which mortar men in the British army use called bracketing. They watched there splashes and adjusted accordingly, they managed to hit the perimeter fence of the HLS (helicopter landing site).

It was clear that the insurgents were fully aware of what are tactics were. IDF, was always followed by a foot patrol, and a casualty was always followed by an air evacuation. The 2 Mercian lads were devastated, these lads were just about to cut out and this. They were at the side of the Mastiff in tears. I was gutted for them. There troop leader came over a Lt Beetleman, his eyes were red raw and he could barely speak. He gathered his troop together and spoke to them. He told them that crying was good and that it was okay to be in bits, it wouldn't be normal otherwise. I didn't know where to look and tried to move away but the lads said to stay, that it could happen to one of our lads in the coming months………….It was just after 1200 on our first day, we had been IDFed twice, an IED and a casualty, welcome to CF Burma, Herrick 16.

INTRODUCTION

"There is no avoiding war, it can only be postponed to the advantage of your enemy."

— Niccolò Machiavelli

"The west have the digital watches but we have the time"

— Mullah Omar (Taliban Commander)

INTRODUCTION

My earliest memory was standing in a crowd with my dad in Milltown cemetery in 1981. I was 4 years old. There were thousands of people there. A man was on a platform speaking to the crowd. Gunshots ring out as masked men fired volleys of shots over a coffin draped with the tricolour. It was the funeral of Bobby Sands. I don't know if I imagine some of it or if my memory has been tricked by news items and YouTube videos I have watched later, but one thing is for sure, I can remember vividly the crowd cheering every time a salvo was fired.

I was born on the 8th of September 1977 in the Royal Victoria Hospital on the Falls Road in Belfast, to my mum Claire, dad John and older brother Sean. My early years were spent living in Andersonstown Cresant, then we moved to a bigger house in Coolnasilla, and when my parents broke up we moved back to Andersonstown Cresant, so that my Mum could be closer to her parents my Granddad Frank and my Granny Margret.

I had a brilliant childhood, up at dawn home at dusk, always exploring with other kids from the area, the bombed buildings, burnt cars and buses, or playing on barricades. A favourite past time of ours was to throw stones at the Army patrols which went through our estate, or abuse them if they had the courage to come through on foot. Even at a young age you knew that something was wrong, and in the eighties in Andersonstown, there was a lot wrong. The biggest recruiter the IRA had were British squaddies, they treated the people of Andersonstown like dirt, and I shed no tears anytime one of them got hit. The Soldiers of the British army who patrolled the streets of Andersonstown were pure evil, they were the bottom rung of society of the UK and they were brutal. The

British thought they could beat the people of Andersonstown into submission but it only toughened our resolve.

At a young age you're very much a product of environment, and by the age of ten, I had witnessed, some of the biggest events of the troubles. 3 men murdered in Milltown cemetery, a loyalist Michael Stone who under the protection of British intelligence tried to assassinate the Sinn Fein leadership at the funeral of the Gibraltar 3. He failed but managed to kill 3 innocent mourners. 5 days later at the funerals of these mourners, the SAS sent 2 undercover soldiers into try again but they were uncovered and both were killed in retaliation.

I was aware that before I was born, my Granddad was shot in the back unarmed as he went to work, by the SAS and that my uncle Thomas was murdered by cowards, a few days before Christmas, with 5 children at home. To a child these are just things in the background and my main concerns were running about with my mates getting up to mischief.

I was quite good in school and passed a lot of GCSEs, but the local Grammar school which my brother was in, refused to allow me to progress there, due to unfounded rumours of what I was doing at the bowling alley in Andersonstown. I joined the Belfast institute for technology at Whiterock, with a mate of mine called Gavin and studied for my A levels in 1 year. Politics and Philosophy. The teacher there was outstanding, Alan Duffield, he treated us like Adults and his love of Greek philosophy was infectious. I passed my A levels with a C in Philosophy and an E in Politics, a full year before my counterparts who left school before me.

I messed around in Belfast for a few years causing mayhem, after that doing courses and taking minor jobs. I kept getting into trouble though and decided that

Belfast wasn't for me. I moved to Dublin with my Brother and had a ball this was the CELTIC Tiger in full roar, I worked in a banking centre full of young people and we had a laugh. Our Sean who was quite successful at the time was planning to go on a tour of Australia, and asked me what I wanted to do. My goal was to tour Europe, so I made arrangements for digs and jobs in Amsterdam, saved up and flew out a few weeks later.

This give me a bit of a travel buzz, and I worked in Pubs, factory's, hotels and farms. Across Europe there is a massive sub-culture of young Irish people, experiencing life before or after they settle down to Uni or get jobs. These were the days before Facebook, but email was available and that's how we all stayed in touch. I went to Belgium, France, Germany worked in a pub in Amsterdam's red light district and ended up working in the hotel trade in Jersey in a few years.

These were brilliant experiences, but I was talking to my mate Gavin who was in University in Liverpool and he told me to apply and come over. I applied to do Single Honours Politics at John Moore University, Liverpool, I did not have the marks to study Philosophy at Liverpool. My goal at this point was to study Politics, finish my course, go home to Ireland and get involved in local Politics. Liverpool was amazing, it was a cultural melting pot and they loved the Irish. The girls were stunning and there was an energy and vibe in the city in the student bars and gyms. Gavin and I had a laugh in Liverpool, but we destroyed ourselves by having girlfriends, I had met Sharon just before starting my course (who I am still with now), and he was living with his girlfriend. Gavin was a year ahead of me and went back home when he finished his course. I graduated with a 2/2 honours Degree, and Sharon and I returned home to live in Ireland with a new arrival, a son who was 2 years old. Sharon had a big family and missed them so Ireland didn't last long, around a year,

we returned to Liverpool. In the next few years I had a

succession of good jobs, a Prison Officer and Personnel

Banking Advisor, but they simply weren't challenging

enough. I was reading a book a week on WW1, WW11,

and studied soviet tank warfare, tactics and the race for

Berlin. The soviets effectively ended WW2 and won the

war against the Germans, with their ruthless approach

and small T34s. I enquired about joining the French

Foreign Legion, as most Catholics from Belfast who

want to join the Army do. But you had to do a straight

commitment of five years, which I couldn't commit to. I

also sent a letter to the Russian Army but never received

a reply. I was debating joining a TA unit in Liverpool

and attended a few times and then the company I was

working for went into 3 month receivership, which

effectively meant that they would lose 70% of their

workforce in 90 days. I spoke to Sharon about joining

the Army, she wasn't keen, but if I wanted to do it, she would support me.

I was torn ideologically about joining the British Army. I had seen first-hand the thuggery of their units on the streets in Andersosntown. The shoot to kill policies and the collusion with the inferior forces of loyalism. I was fascinated by Tanks though and Tank warfare and if Sinn Fein could sit in a British Government I could join the Army.

I went into the careers office in Liverpool and they give me some info and booked me into a few numeracy and literacy tests. The careers office lads tried to get me to join the infantry, and explained I could be at phase 1 in a few weeks. I scored quite highly in the British Army Recruitment Battery (BARB) and had every non-medical and musical role open to me. I was torn between Intelligence and the Royal Armoured Core, and even at one stage was given a date for Chicksands. A recruiting Sargent called Sgt Molyneaux was a 1RTR soldier and he explained there history and job-role. They were the unit I was aiming for and was happy to go to their cap badge.

To join the army you have to swear an oath of allegiance to the Queen and Her successors, similar to the oath you have to say in order to stand in Parliament. I went into the careers office and spoke to a late entry Royal Engineers Major who told me that the oath wasn't worth the paper it was written on and I didn't have to say it if I didn't want too. I asked him why and he told me that the Army had changed. The oath states

__"I (your name here) swear by Almighty God that I will be faithful and bear true allegiance to Her Majesty Queen Elizabeth the Second, Her Heirs and Successors and that I will as in duty bound honestly and faithfully defend Her Majesty, Her Heirs and Successors in Person, Crown and Dignity against all__

<u>enemies and will observe and obey all orders of Her</u>

<u>Majesty, Her Heirs and Successors and of the</u>

<u>Generals and Officers set over me.</u>"

The reason he said it didn't matter was the Army was under fire from a succession of mistreatment and abuse cases. Iraq and Afghanistan had been mismanaged epically. Junior soldiers were brutalising the civilian population of these countries on orders from the rank in their units. When the junior soldiers were getting done they were using the oath as an excuse. They didn't release that if you kill someone no orders or rank structure are going to protect you. He also told me that the biggest fear the British Army had was a truth and reconciliation commission for Northern Ireland which would destroy the government of the day and bankrupt the Army.

Once they realise your serious things moved quite quickly, I passed my assessments and soon got a date for Phase 1 training at ATR Bassingbourn 15th of November 2009, and joined "the bastards Army". Phase 1 was nothing like I expected it to be. The Army had changed due to recent deaths and suicides in training. Phase 1 was managed well, with approachable Corporals and Platoon Staff. I was a complete drill mong and just could not get the hang of it. The platoon Sgt Paul Graham (Bomber) told me to manage a halt and salute and as a tankie that was all you need. There was a Para Sgt up the stairs who used to come down and talk to me. Sgt Dave Phillips was black with a stutter but hard as nails, and a cracking bloke. He was really interested in the troubles and couldn't understand why the IRA had given up when they were so close to obtaining a united Ireland. This attitude was prevalent amongst the old hands in the Army. I never understood why the ceasefire stuck when one or two more spectaculars could have secured enough disharmony in the British voting public to hand us back to the South.

In Phase one all you have to do is not cheek the staff and try and show that you took on board what they say. All the training team wanted to see was a good attitude and that you listened. There was a lot of reverse racism in phase 1, commonwealth African soldiers, pulled out of everything, exercises, boot runs, tabs, and still made it through, were lots of English lads would get back squaded for the same thing. The lads who didn't make it through, just tried to coast and back chatted the staff when asked to do something. They were caught out pretty quickly and just explained that they were not suited to the army and if they couldn't behave in training, you would have future problems at Regiment.

I passed out with a parade on the drill square, Sharon came down. I turned up at phase 2 which was in Bovington. This is a really nice part of the country and I enjoyed my time here. Phase 1 teaches you basic conventional Army drills, weapons, dress, drill, rank structure, conventional tactics, and phase 2 trains you for your trade training, signals, Tank driving, Tank Gunnery. The Corporals in phase 1 training are normally the best in there regiment, the fittest, best kitted out, sharpest creases, most experienced top ten of the reg. Phase 2 is the complete opposite the Corporals who are known as full screws were a mess. One full screw from the household cavalry, didn't shave or iron his kit, or clean his boots. The full screws were all biffed up with lazy attitudes, always dodging any work. Not one of them could pass any of the basic military fitness tests, or give trustable advice. I limited my dealings with them and cracked on with my trade training. At a trooper level all you have to do is be in the right place at the right time in the right dress. I passed my trade training at a rapid pace, and D and M tank training was probably the best course I have ever done. An ex RTR soldier called Mr Stone (Rocky), took us for training and he was awesome. I came top of his class and to be honest I was sad to move on. Tank training in the sun, in Bovington is unreal and I would recommend it to anyone.

I passed out at a faster rate than the lads I arrived with and completed my MATTs (Military Annul Training Tests) training with a different group of lads. MATTs was really good, a complete refreshment of phase 1 and phase 2. I touched lucky, I had 2 weeks off, before reg. I spoke to Sgt Molyneux who told me that A squadron 1 RTR had a month off in 3 weeks' time, and told me not to bother turning up until 01/09/2010, as it was only the start of July, I ended up with close to 2 months off.

MATTs

Military Annual Training Tests (MATTs) are a series of annual tests that every soldier is required to complete in order to stay current. They are tested at 3 different levels (funnily enough Level 1, Level 2 and Level 3) and generally speaking you will be tested at Level 2 every year unless you are deploying on Operations (in which case you will be trained to Level 1) or the Chain of Command (CoC) has reduced the requirement to Level 3. There are different tests within each MATT and the Level you are training at determines which of the tests you will take for each MATT you are required to complete (at Level 3 for example MATTs 4 & 5 are not tested at all).

The subjects covered in each MATT are as follows:

MATT 1 - Personal Weapon Training

MATT 2 - Fitness

MATT 3 - Battlefield Casualty Drills (BCD)

MATT 4 - Chemical, Biological, Radiological, Nuclear (CBRN)

MATT 5 - Navigation

MATT 6 - Values and Standards (V&S)

MATT 7 - Law of Armed Conflict (LOAC)

MATT 8 - Survive, Evade, Resist, Extract (SERE)

MATT 9 - Counter Improvised Explosive Device (C-IED)

When you will be tested on each of these will vary depending on where you complete your Phase 1 training but the Training Programmes on this page will give you some guidance. On completion of Phase 1 you willl have been tested at some point in all MATTs with the exception of MATT 2 - Fitness (though you will have been constantly improving your fitness throughout Phase 1 and will have been assessed as you progress the formal MATT 2 tests are not completed during Phase 1).

REGIMENT

"The 1st Royal Tank Regiment is based at RAF Honington in Suffolk with A Squadron being posted to Warminster. It has a distinguished history, which has seen it break the German line at Cambrai in 1917, hold out against Rommel in the North African Desert as part of the Desert Rats and it repelled repeated Communist attacks in Korea in1951.The Regiment has returned to the armoured role after handing over the specialist Chemical, Biological, Radiological and Nuclear reconnaissance role to the RAF Regiment, a role which it has pioneered and developed since 1999. It now operates a range of vehicles which includes the Challenger 2 Main Battle Tank, a formidable machine designed to destroy enemy vehicles and punch a hole in their defences.

The Regiment has served in Afghanistan, mounted in several different variants of the British Army's new fleet of Protected Patrol Vehicles. Tankies once again demonstrated their adaptability and utility when handling these vehicles in difficult terrain, protecting the Afghan people in the face of a determined enemy.

In recent months the First has returned from Helmand province in support of the Infantry and equipped with the Mastiff vehicle. Other units facilitated the handover of forces deployed on Op HERRICK, and a small team deployed as dog handlers. The Regimental Headquarters deployed to fill a number of jobs in the Brigade Headquarters.

A Squadron remain the armoured squadron of the Land Warfare Centre Battlegroup; providing support to all major exercises on Salisbury Plain Training Area using Challenger 2 and CVR(T) Scimitar, as well as training the armoured crews of the future.

1 RTR recruits from Scotland and the North West of England, giving the regiment a very distinct character, unlike any other in the Royal Armoured Corps. With the majority of their soldiers coming from Liverpool and Glasgow, football is a passion!

To reflect their Scottish links they have a Pipes and Drums. The Pipes and Drums are primarily tank soldiers who decide that they would like to try their hand at something different. This summer they were seen performing at the Edinburgh Festival and Military Tattoo.

They have sent soldiers to Canada, Cyprus, the USA and Thailand as well as all the British Army operational zones.

On the sporting front the regiment is currently the Army cycling champions, and has in recent years won the

Royal Armoured Corps Rugby Cup two years running.

Winter sports are equally popular and two soldiers from 1 RTR are currently training with the British Olympic Team for the two-man bob event." (1RTR Website)

1RTR at this stage was split in 2. 1RTR A squadron was a training squadron based in Warminster, and was used for training Tank commanders for main battle tanks and reconnaissance courses for formation reconnaissance and close recce. It was right next to the Salisbury Plain Training Area (SPTA). The rest of the regiment had a CBRN (Chemical Biological Radiological Nuclear) role and were based with the RAF up in Honington in Norfolk. Not one person I have spoken to has ever been positive about the CBRN role, I never did it so it's hard for me to comment. The main gripe was that the role was shared with the RAF regiment, who historically have never been seen by any branches of the Armed forces as real soldiers. RAF pilots, loaders, door gunners, air traffic control, med evac teams, police all do serious soldering and are vital to the security of the country. The RAF regiment man Sangers around airport and are considered by the three branches of the Armed forces to be REMFs, a term of derision used by front line soldiers to describe those in cushy jobs in the rear. It is short for 'Rear Echelon Mother Fucker' and is familiar to most troopers who have been involved in any conflict.

"This place is a nightmare. I wish to be a REMF," said the American soldier during the 1968 Battle for Hue.

That is it. In the Army we always STAG on at bases, but we also go on the ground, capture detainees, and search for IEDs, take on the enemy, vehicle checkpoints, easily too many roles to mention. The RAF regiment do 4 month tours of large bases and don't go across the wire.

The Army despise them for their cowardice, to sit back and take a wage for effectively doing a civilian's job is unethical. With 1RTR being attached to them it sullied the regiments good name.

The accommodation at Warminster was some of the worst I had ever seen. It was 4 man rooms that were falling apart with no TV signal or working electrics. I was put into Military Transport (MT) when I arrived. This is viewed as the worst role in a tank unit and attracts bad soldiers who are only there for a wage and Commonwealth. Every one there was on a biff, overweight and long term in rank, ten year lance jacks, 20 year full screws. I was embarrassed to be put there and asked for a transfer to an MBT (Main Battle Tank) unit. It was denied at first, so I then complained like fuck and they moved me to Reconnaissance Troop. The lads here were viewed as the best at Reg, fit, and switched on and ambitious, but these lads were just coasting as well. There were some bad ones here who thought the Army owed them, a 7 year trooper was there who had dodged 3 tours and cried every time he was shouted at, and a fat lazy Scottish lance jack who point blank refused to do any work. The Troop Sgt was called Johno and was from around the corner from me in Liverpool. He was a JTAC (Joint Tactical Air Controller) and had cracking war stories from Afghanistan. At Reg you are expected not to talk about your experiences in theatre, I don't know why this is, I think it's because people are jealous who have took the easy option throughout their career, the ones who have never fired a round. I loved listening to Johno, you could see he put himself at great personal risk.

Recce troop was insanely busy, we spent almost every week out on the SPTA (Salisbury Plain Training Area) training commanders in formation and close recce. We used CVRT (Close Vehicle Reconnaissance Tracked) vehicles which are like baby tanks. Being new I was really keen, so I enjoyed being out on exercise. I was ten months in when the 2 IC Captain Holloway phoned me and asked if I would like to go to Afghanistan as a dog handler on op beak. He explained the role was to search and confirm IED finds for infantry sections. This role simply didn't interest me, there were 30 spaces and one of my mates Russ in recce troop went for it. The roles locations sounded good as you trained in Germany and America, but it must be one of the most dangerous out there. The OP Beak lads were going to be thrashed and taken completely out of their comfort zone, I thought this is going to end in disaster. A few days later the SM gathered everyone in a circle on the tank park and asked for 30 volunteers to boost G Sqns Mastiff tour in 4 months. 96 people applied, I said no, as I had no unconventional warfare training, and couldn't see how I could learn it in 4 months. 5 lads in recce troop who volunteered pulled out 24 hours later. There excuses were lies which were boarding on cowardice. The 96 people dropped to around 20 the next day.

Each troop had to provide a certain number for the tour so I was told due to all the withdrawals that I was being mobilised to go on it. From the start it was rushed, I was unsure what my role was going to be, whether I was going on armour, on foot, or on a specialist role such as op beak. A squadron put 18 guys together from across the troops and sent them for pre-deployment training in Honington.

PRE-

DEPLOYMENT

TRAINING

"If it's natural to kill, how come men have to go into training to learn how?"

Joan Baez

PRE-DEPLOYMENT TRAINING 04/10/2011

*"Pre-Deployment Training (PDT) is essential to
properly prepare for duties in foreign, often hostile
countries. As well as exercises to develop their physical
fitness, PDT also includes training to develop
organisational, leadership and decision making skills,
all of which help soldiers work as a team and under
pressure.*

*Pre-deployment training is intense. It not only
reinforces and refines the skills they've acquired so far,
but also ensures they're fully trained in the use of any*

specific vehicles, technology or weapons systems they'll
be using on tour. We also prepare them to deal
correctly and appropriately with the local nationals
they are likely to meet." (MOD Website)

I wasn't happy from the start, we got moved to RAF
Honington to join G Squadron and take part in their
training. Honington was worse than everyone made out
it was a mess and the RAF hated us. G squadron was
broken down into 4 troops, 09, 10, 11 and 12 Troop.
Each troop was 18 people strong, 2 sections of 9 which
could then be broken down into 3, 3 man Mastiff crews.
My Troop was 11 Troop. Each Troop was being
attached to different infantry units who were going out
across different AOs (areas of operations) across
Helmand in Herrick 16. Herrick was the codename
under which British operations in Afghanistan have
operated under since 2002. Iraq was called TELIC. 11
Troop were attached to the 1st Royal Welsh Fusiliers, a

light infantry unit based in Chester. G squadron treated the lads who came from A squadron like shit, we were always moving rooms and having no structured accommodation, whereas the other G Squadron lads were on the pigs back. I was attached to G Sqn for 4 months before tour and moved room 5 times. The other G Sqn lads never shared any information with us and literally just sucked up to rank. A few of the lads were okay, Mick Williams, Tom Drasiey and Bondy were shocked at how we were treated.

Every other Troop apart from 11 troop knew what their job role was, when they were going, what date they were coming back, and what there R and R dates were. Our Troop hierarchy was a troop Sgt called Craig Causer and a troop leader Mr McCullough who was in the army for less time than I was. They had absolutely no information concerning the tour and it was like pulling teeth trying to get anything from them. The Troop was broken up like this

Section 1

Crews

Commander	Gunner	Driver

Lt McCullough (Troop leader), L/Cpl Murray (Minty)
Trooper McCartan

Cpl Molyneaux (Molly) Trooper McGeachin (Bob)
Trooper Suthers

L/Cpl McNeill (Macca) Trooper O Connor (Des)
Cfn Gwilliam

Section 2

Sgt Causer, Trooper Reid

Trooper Doyle

Cpl Walker (Jay)   Trooper Tucker
Trooper Sansom

L/Cpl Morris (Mo)   Trooper Biggs
Trooper Brown

I was glad I wasn't in Craig's section as he lost his temper every time he was asked a question. I had seen this type of man management before, from lazy ass phase 2 full screws. If Mr McCullough didn't know the answer to a question he would investigate and get back to you with the response that he was told. If Craig didn't know the answer he would either make something up or start screaming, that you didn't need to know that. The main problem with my section is that it lacked any real leadership or experience. Also Macca and Molly hated each other and simply divided the Troop. I got on with both individually and they were good lads, but when they were with each other you felt like you had to take sides, which was always uncomfortable. The Troop hierarchy was fully aware of this but done nothing to counteract it. Jay and Craig were mates so looked after each other.

The pre-deployment training was laughable, because we didn't know what we were doing we couldn't prioritise our training. The 1RWF wouldn't tell us if we were on Mastiffs or on foot. 2 people out of our troop had been to Afghanistan before, Mo went on Vikings as the previous troop leader's driver, and Molly had done a few months on the Vikings also but fucked the tour off half way through. At one stage we were walking around a hanger on camp with a valon (IED metal Detector) with no batteries. Pre deployment training is a series of field exercises which you have to pass in order for your unit to be declared operationally deployable. We had missed Kenya and Canada and just done the shit ones in the UK. What G Sqn and the rest of 1RTR didn't understand was that it was fucking freezing in the winter in the UK and fucking roasting in Afghanistan in the summer. The training defied any reason or logic.

The unit does a live firing range (Hide and Lid), a CFX (Afghanistan based exercise, combat drills etc), a live firing exercise in south Wales, and another CFX, then one last Afghan based exercise. On top of the field exercises you have to pass personal fitness tests, and as we thought we were going on Mastiffs we had to do the vehicle training in Bovington and Leconfield. All these are assessed by independent army assessors called DS. I was almost killed on exercise due to Molly having a ND and hitting the wall next to me. Craig covered it up though so as not to make the Troop look bad. The 1RWF had also went on exercise to Kenya and Canada and completed 18 months continual training for deployment.

We were attached to the 1RWF we thought as Mastiff crews, when we went on exercise in Stanta with them in Feb 12, a month before deployment that changed. Their arrogant OC took 30 seconds of his time to come and brief us. He explained that we were slotting into 18 TA places they couldn't fill and that we were being spread across his company into different sections, as independent soldiers. This effectively meant that we would each be separated from our crews and troops.

This shocked everyone and Mr McCullough and Craig lost control of their Troop. The fact that they didn't know at this stage that this was happening was bad leadership. I had a right go at both of them and everyone agreed with me. They had both been lying to the Troop, on what they were guessing would happen. Jay went sick with his knee and asked to be taken off the exercise.

On the exercise the 1RWF broke us down into our sections, and made us carry their weight, ladders, stretchers, ECM suite and section ammunition (ECM stands for Electronic Counter Measure and is a system to block signals to detonate IEDs through laser, infa-red etc.). They blatantly were taking the piss. I was with the section I was deploying with and took an instant dislike to the troop Sgt, a Sgt Dean. Sgt Dean had just been promoted and was a phase 1 corporal and he used his rank to protect him and to talk down to people. They were shocking on exercise and had to be retested 3 times, on one of the harder phases of the exercise, which my troop completed first time and got top marks for. The problem with the 1RWF wasn't that they were bad soldiers, it was that they thought they knew it all and therefore didn't respond well to training. Because 11 Troop was full of relatively new lads, we listened and took on board all aspects of training absorbing the points emphasized to us, the DS loved us. The Welsh had been out on the Herrick's 7 times and only lost two guys, which was an amazing record. There last tour however had been 3 years ago and the insurgents were fluid, always updating their drills. So the DS staff on Stanta training area in Thetford were training us for current threats, and for what we would face in the summer.

Jay had went back to camp with his knee as an excuse and requested to see the G SQN OC and SM. Jay explained to the OC a Major Ford of what had been taking place with the Welsh. Major Ford was simply not a man to suffer fools and honestly had no idea what was going on. Craig and Mr McCullough had been telling him everything was going to plan and had been hiding the difficulties that the Troop was facing. Jay had taken a massive risk and I had respect for him for doing it.

Major Ford spoke to our CO Lt Col Brittan, who when he found out spoke directly to the CO of the 1RWF. Our 1RTR hierarchy was going to pull 11 troops tour if we were not given access to Mastiff vehicles. 1RWF had trained for 18 months, were we had 4 months training. The Welsh had got on quickly to Craig and Mr McCullough's inexperience and basically told them that we would be working for them, when our CO found out what was going on the message was clear, 11 Troop would be working with you as an attachment not for you, as grunts.

Craig and Mr McCullough were letting the Welsh lead them, what they didn't understand was, that the 1RWF were untrustworthy. I had spoken to the Welsh lads on exercise and 40% of their regiment had left in just over a year, because of how badly it was being run. Not only that they were desperately undermanned and could not fulfil their commitment for Herrick 16. They were bolstering their manpower through TA, reservists and spares from other regiments. 2 Mercian's were out in CF Burma on a winter tour which is traditionally a quiet time in Afghanistan with 300 manpower the 1RWF were bringing 180, in the summer for what was the most kinetic AO out of every Herrick.

Craig was raging that he had been caught out not communicating concern's with the G SQN hierarchy, but still tried to claim some sort of victory that we were on Mastiffs. I was constantly argumentative during pre-deployment training as I was the only one who hadn't volunteered to go. Craig spoke to me and told me that having concerns was fine, and it was easy to fly off the handle and make demands as a Trooper, but as a

Sergeant you had to compromise and work with people, I told him that all information should be shared and there should be a dividing line between us and the Welsh, and that compromising with these people wouldn't work as they would just take and take.

CF Burma didn't exist in the British press, as it was just another name for Sangan the most dangerous area of Helmand. Sangan was supposed to be handed back to the Americans, so the MOD just kept changing its name and telling the press lads were getting hit elsewhere.

A Mastiff is a heavily armoured, 6 x six-wheel-drive patrol vehicle which carries eight troops, plus three crew. It is currently on its third variation. Mastiff 1, 2, 3 and a REME variant the Wolfhound.
It is suitable for road patrols and convoys and is the newest in a range of protected patrol vehicles being used for operations. Mastiff has a maximum speed of 90kph, is armed with the latest weapon systems,

including a 7.62mm general purpose machine gun, 12.7mm heavy machine gun or 40mm automatic grenade launcher, or a 50 Cal long range weapon system. These wheeled patrol vehicles have a less intimidating profile than tracked vehicles and give commanders on the ground in Afghanistan more options to deal with the threats they are facing. They have Bowman radios and electronic countermeasures and are fitted with additional armour beyond the standard level to ensure they have the best possible protection.

Improvements on the Mastiff include:

- Bigger axles and up-rated suspension
- Increased electrical power from the alternator 400A vs 200A
- Increased crew capacity 2 + 8 as opposed to 2 + 6

- Increased CES/stowage locations

- Blast attenuating seats

- Fold up seats allowing easier stowage if the
  vehicle is not full of crew

- New situational awareness system incorporating
  a thermal imager for the driver

The vehicles are based on the US Cougar made by
Force Protection, with UK integration work carried
out by NP Aerospace, in Coventry. They have a V
shaped hull which reduces blast impact by sending the
explosion off in different directions. The fixtures and
fittings are brass which melts in the heat of a blast. So
rather than ripping the hull to bits, the fittings will fly
off leaving the hull intact. A Mastiff operates with a
commander gunner and driver. A minimum of 2 go
out on the ground at any one team. The lead Mastiff
has an attachment called a choker/mine roller. This is
an extension around 1.5meters long and 3.5 tons in

weight. It is a series of wheels which set off pressure plate IEDs, which in theory blow the choker up, which is designed to blow apart. The choker is always placed on the leading vehicle as it would not make sense on the rear. The insurgents had got around this by setting the pressure plates and charge away from each other, which created more ground sign, so commanders found them easier to spot.

The atmosphere in the Troop became a lot more positive, being on Mastiffs greatly reduced the threat and there was little cause for complaint. Our pre-deployment leave was coming up and everyone was looking forward to it.

THE MISSION

Our objectives in Afghanistan were to maintain security on the Main Supply Route (MSR) from Geresh to Sangan. We were to patrol a 25km stretch of road called the 611 and conduct a series of VP checks along the route. We had to hand over the CPs and

bases to our Afghan partners the ANSF, (Afghanistan

National Security Forces)

07/03/2012 PRE-DEPLOYMENT LEAVE

I got a phone call from my mate Rourkie, who was on exercise on the SPTA at around 0730. I thought he was having a laugh so I ignored it. He kept phoning and I eventually answered. He was training with the 3 York's who we shared a base with in Warminster. He told me that a major incident involving a warrior crew had taken place and that 6 soldiers had been killed. My phone didn't stop all morning, as we were leaving for Bastion on the 10th, a wave of panic had set in with my Parents and other members of the Troop. The news that had been broadcast was saying that the 6 lads were MIA (missing in action).

The warrior had hit a massive IED on a familiarisation patrol, and the ammunition ignited, hundreds of 30mm shells destroyed everything, the MOD had to class them as MIA as there was no trace of them. " *The six soldiers, five from the newly arrived 3rd Bn The Yorkshire Regiment and one from 1st Bn the Duke of Lancaster's Regiment, were driving in the desert at dusk when the Warrior was hit by what has been*

described as an "enormous" bomb" (The Telegraph).

This was a huge blow for the 3 York's and devastated

the small town of Warminster. Sharon came home

from work early and we went out for dinner. I spent

the next few days taking my son swimming and to the

cinema and park. I cooked Sharon dinner and watched

a few films with red wine, just having a laugh. When I

left to go back to camp it was hard, Sharon was in

tears. I picked up 2 of my troop, Suthers and Des and

we went down to base for deployment. They told me

that Craig and McCullough had covered up a violent

assault on a Trooper by an NCO and swept it under

the carpet. I refused to believe this as I always thought

McCullough if anything was straight. When I found

out this was true I lost almost all respect for him

11/03/2012 ONE HOUR STOP OVER RAF

AKROTIR CYPRUS

We stopped off for one hour at RAF Akrotir for refuelling on our way to Camp Bastion. I had a shave and brushed my teeth in the washroom. I was sitting with Jay when he had a call from his wife. An American soldier had left his base and killed 16 members of the same family in an Afghan village in Khandahar. Staff Sgt Robert Bales walked out of his PB armed to the teeth and shot, men women and children who were in bed, for no apparent reason. There were mass demonstrations and a huge anti-ISAF backlash devcloping in the towns and villages.

"A US soldier in Afghanistan has killed at least 16 civilians and wounded five after entering their homes in Kandahar province, senior local officials say.

He left his military base in the early hours of the morning and opened fire in at least two homes; women and children were among the dead.

Nato said it was investigating the "deeply regrettable incident".

Anti-US sentiment is already high in Afghanistan after US soldier's burnt copies of the Koran last month"
(BBC)

The Afghan President ordered all ISAF forces not to patrol in villages or enter population centres. There was no way this would be feasible as the insurgents would just use the local population as cover and mount attacks from mosques and schools.

12/03/2012 – 21/03/2012 RECEPTION STAGING ONWARD INTEGRATION (RSOI)

When you arrive in Camp Bastion, Newly arrived soldiers in Afghanistan wait at the Reception, Staging and Onward Integration (RSOI) Area at Camp Bastion in Afghanistan before onward deployment.

Reception Staging Onward Integration (RSOI) is a system designed to help train, acclimatise and move soldiers to their deployed location in Helmand. Soldiers conduct 2-7 days RSOI dependant on their role.

Topics covered during the training are Counter-IED, health issues, cultural awareness and a host of other subjects. The training is long and tiring but is the best training prior to the real thing the soldiers will experience.

This is all well and good but the lads who were taking the RSOI were 1RTR D SQN and most of them had

--

never been to Afghanistan before or been on tour before so the lads taking the packages hadn't a clue. 2 1RTR Lance jacks were supervising the rodette, a roll cage which mimicked the rolling of an AFV when it was hit. There was a rattling in the rodette but they carried on with their drills. When they opened the back doors, they found the rattling to be a fragmentation grenade which hadn't been checked in. Eight men are in the cage at any one time. 1RTR had effectively sent all the undeployable biffs from the regiment on RSOI, a risk free way of earning a medal. Being based in Camp Bastion is like being in Catterick or Aldershot, without the alcohol, it is like a large garrison. We are the first people to be critical of the RAF Regiment for their REMF (Rear Echelon Mother Fuckers) status, and then we send a squadron to do the most embarrassing job in the Army.

When you arrive for RSOI you are meant to have a zero day. This is a day where you sort all your administration out, weapons, armour, etc. We arrived at 0230 and were informed by a 1RTR major that our first brief would be at 0530 and that are zero day was cancelled due to a mix up by the RSOI staff. The Welsh lads hated us for this. Everyone was exhausted throughout the briefs and kept falling asleep, this just entailed us getting bollacked by RSOI staff who had had a full night's sleep.

During our RSOI there was an attack on the airfield, as a direct response to the American killing the civilians, a LEC (locally employed civilian), strapped a SBIED to himself and fired down Camp Bastian runway, but it went off early and partially exploded.

"An Afghan man who crashed a stolen vehicle on to the runway at Camp Bastion as US defence Secretary Leon Panetta arrived there has died of his injuries.

Lt Gen Curtis Scaparotti, the deputy commander of American forces in Afghanistan, said the man died this morning of severe burns.

He said the driver apparently had a container of fuel in the vehicle, which ignited during yesterday's crash at the British airfield in Helmand province in southern Afghanistan.

Lt Gen Scaparotti said the driver had been heading towards a group of marines.

The driver travelled at high speed and crashed into a ditch near the ramp where Mr Panetta's plane was going to park. No one in the defence secretary's party was hurt.

The drama at Camp Bastion is believed to be linked to an earlier incident, which left a British serviceman with minor injuries." (BFPS News)

Under interrogation the LEC said that there were 6 more attack's planned by the LECs in Bastion, so we had to wear armour everywhere and carry our rifles.

The Taliban issued a statement asking all there fighters to attack all ISAF forces and intensify their operations. They were using the resentment brought about by the Americans murder spree to garner support, and it was working. The yanks were also caught burning copies of the Quran, which was just brilliant.

Our directives and objectives in Afghanistan were changing by the minute, and President Obama and Prime Minster Cameron announced a full withdrawal from Afghanistan, by 2014. The threat level was the highest it had ever been, and our briefs were now about staying alive and CP security when working with our Afghan partners the Afghan National Security Forces (ANSF), who were saying that we would be paying in blood for the village attacks.

We were meant to be living with these people in a few days, seasoned infanteers where looking worried, the ANSF had opened up a few times on British soldiers when there back was turned, for minor offence, what would happen when we were killing entire families in their sleep.

We were preparing to go on the ground when a sand storm took up. I had never seen anything like this before. All flights and all non-essential movement were cancelled. The sand storm was like something out of a film, you literally could not see the hand in front of your face. Everything looked pixelated or scrambled. We were mobilised to go during the sand storm and travelled to a holding centre in a small mini bus, the song that was being played over the radio was wild boys by Duran Duran.

MARCH

"There is no instance of a nation benefitting from prolonged warfare."

Sun Tzu

21/03/2012 DAY ONE/ 2 MERCIAN'S

We were already 3 days late for the vehicle handover due to the sandstorm engulfing Helmand. All Flights were grounded, and all patrols cancelled due to the inability to provide air support or casualty extractions by helicopter.

The 2 Mercian's got sick of waiting and drove from FOB Ouellette to Camp Bastian in Mastiff armoured fighting vehicles, a 4 hour vehicle Journey down the 611 and onto the 601, effectively from Sangan, through Gerash, Lash and to the safety of Bastian. The rip is possibly the most dangerous time when you're on tour the bases have double the manpower, the lads who are leaving and the lads who are staying. Inexperience and experience, there's more movements from the FOBS and checkpoints providing double the targets. Everything is rushed and no one has a clue.

As only a handful of people could be carried in the Mastiff, positions were prioritised due to importance of role. Effectively Mastiff Driver and commander, the gunners could sit this one out, as a commander could double as a gunner due to the positions of the crews. I was duel trained, a driver and gunner but some of the lads were just gunners, which was harsh on the drivers as the gunners always got breaks were the drivers got thrashed.

We waited for hours in a holding room, in the 1RWFs admin area of Bastian. There was a TV, books and some comfy chairs. Op minimise was on due to an incident to the south of Garesh so we couldn't phone home or go on the internet, conversation was minimal, nobody seemed to be talking "It is called Operation Minimise, an order from brigade headquarters in southern Afghanistan to restrict communications. British troops in Helmand province dread Op Minimise. They know commanders will be phoning the UK, a call that will lead to a family being told that their son or daughter is dead". I fell asleep on my kit which was a Bergan and day sack. I can remember people being nervous and of course apprehensive.

The 2 Mercian's were late, and by late I mean hours late, they were meant to be there at 2000 to brief us and explain the route, it was now 0030 and there was nothing from them. OP minimise come off, and I phoned Sharon and my Mum, they were both concerned and the previous week's incident in the Warrior was in everyone's minds.

The 2 Mercian's pulled up and the inevitable bad Army shout of hurry up and wait was called. We rushed into a car park were there 4 Mastiff 2 armoured wagons and waited around for about an hour. The lads were sound, tired but sound. They had come down in 2 man crews, just driver and commander, this was to maximise space.

This is a massive risk due to there being no Barmaed team. The biggest threat in Afghanistan is improvised explosive devices (IEDs), the Barmaed team is a makeup of 5 guys, a commander and 4 valon men. The valon is a variation of a metal detector which searches for component parts of IEDs. The 611 and 601 are tarmacked roads, just black asphalt similar to UK roads, it is easy to spot something on them, but this is bad drills.

At vulnerable points the Barmaed team go out and go into a series of drills which search for different IEDs, to not carry a team during a sand storm is risky and to be honest fucking stupid. We broke down into sets of five and loaded our kit onto wagons. I jumped in the back of a Mastiff with 4 other RTR lads. This is the first time I had ever sat down while wearing a protective nappy an essential item of kit for soldiers on foot patrol, but an idiotic peace of kit if you're sitting in a Mastiff. If a blast can pierce the armour of a Mastiff I can't imagine the nappy to provide much protection.

Everyone was silent and awake in the back, all I could see were the glow in the dark directional arrows which point to the exits in case you get blown over into water. We stopped periodically for short periods of time, 2 of the lads wanted to go outside for a smoke, but Jay explained to them that if they thought they were going to jump out the back of the wagon in the middle of Afghanistan in a sand storm to have a smoke, it simply would not take place. I was in the back with my mate Jay and a few of the younger lads in the troop, Sano, Brown and Suthers.

The journey was uncomfortable, I drifted in and out hearing bits over the net in bursts. The 2 Mercian HQ in FOB Ouellette were clearly worried about the journey. It didn't feel real in the back of that vehicle, it still felt as if I was waiting for something to happen.

We got to FOB Ouellette late or early, it was hard to decide. It was after 0500. We arranged to take over the wagons at 0830 next to the REME (Royal Electrical Mechanical Engineers or Ruins Every Mechanical Engine) workshop. We went to the transit room and got our heads down. It was freezing. I always imagined Afghanistan to be warm all year round, but there was patches of snow still in places and this was March. Maybe it was to do with altitude, I don't know. When I woke up the next morning, the sandstorm had stopped and the sun was blinding. I got my first look at FOB Ouellette, it was a complete dive, perched on top of what could only be described as large sand dunes.

I spoke to A Company Sgt Major Mills. He welcomed me and explained that I would be a big part of the rip, essentially I would be working with the 2 Mercian's, ripping there lads out of the checkpoints, observation posts, patrol bases in CF Burma and ripping his lads in. This meant that I would learn the AO pretty quickly. It also meant that I would be one of the busiest people in CF Burma.

I went for breakfast in the morning with Mr McCullough (The Boss), who was the troop leader and the commander of the crew on my wagon. I went to the REME and met up with my counterparts in 2 Mercian, the lads were massive. I imagined after a 7 month tour for the lads to be decimated, but they told me they made a makeshift gym in their checkpoint and smashed the weights out using performance enhancers, bought from Americans. Molly and Suthers were there also taking over there vehicle. They were part of a crew. As I was with the Boss, I imagined I would be doing the handover on my own.

A vehicle handover is where you sign for your wagon and all the tools, weaponry, signals, spares and ECM equipment on the wagon. All the tools and associated equipment is laid out in a line at the side of the wagon, the person who you are taking over from will have the vehicle docs which will list the items attached to the vehicle and will call out the names of the items. The person taking over the wagon will then place the items on the wagon, therefore knowing what he is signing for. With a Challenger 2 main battle tank, this can take hours, but the Mastiff is not nearly as complicated.

We were doing the handover in FOB Ouellette Tank Park, which was nicknamed IDF central. The 2 Mercian lads seen I was doing it on my own and came over to help. They explained the job that they had been doing. Their main role was to do daily vulnerable point (VP) checks along the 611, so the Americans could have easy access of a main supply route from Sangan to Lashkar Gah. They explained that they had done 9 foot patrols in total over the 7 months, due to the risk of sniper fire and IEDs. They explained that there had been one killed in action up from their checkpoint on the 611, a young Private named Matthew Haseldin, 21 who was killed by sniper fire on 03rd of November 2011, *"Private Matthew Haseldin, from 2nd Battalion The Mercian Regiment, had been in the Army for just a few months when he was shot while 'standing firm' against an insurgent attack in the Nahr-e Saraj district of Helmand province on November 3" (Daily Mail)*. I had seen his name on a small gold plaque on a mount for a cross by the entrance to the ops room, it was on its own. After that they had cancelled the foot patrols. Also 3 lads had been hit by IEDs and they had 3 mobility kills of the Mastiff.

To be honest it didn't sound that bad. Whoosh, whoosh, whoosh, the Mercian's dragged me into the back of the Mastiff, locked the doors and hatch, There was a succession of 3 explosions, one 25 yards away from our vehicle. The Taliban had fired three Chinese Rockets into the FOB.The IDF alarm was blaring and people were running for hard cover all over the place. When IDF hits the drill is to lie down on your belly, hands over your eyes, and mouth open, or find hard cover. The shrapnel the shell makes when it hits the ground explodes in a funnel shape, so will hit you at height. The insurgents had used the cover of the sand storm to dig themselves in to different positions around the FOB. One of the LECs (locally employed civilians), had obviously tipped them off, that there was mass movement on camp, and it would be a good time to fire.

A 2 Mercian's Captain came over to get a section of lads together to go out on a quick foot patrol, to find the firing points. The lads that were with me, stayed to help with the handover. I carried on and signed for the wagon. My kit insurance would have easily hit the roof, if they were aware that a Trooper was signing for what could easily be £500,000 worth of kit, a used Mastiff 2 much cost a fortune, the signals kit, 2 GPMGs, the tools and the ECM, I wasn't comfortable doing it. Wee Des the only Gunner that got dicked to come up, and didn't bother helping came and got me for lunch, it was around 1130.

Mr McCullough met us and we queued for scoff. The lunch room was packed and it was hard to get a seat. We had only just sat down and a loud explosion shook the entire camp, you could feel the vibration in your body. Everyone thought it was more IDF and the place went mental. Hard cover was right next to the cookhouse and we dived in there. This was our first day on the ground and it was not yet 1200. I was stunned and then I heard someone speaking in derogatory terms about the Irish Rugby team. I turned around and my best mate from phase 1 training was there Thomas Warner, and why a Welsh man was discussing rugby I will never know. He was leaving the same day that I had arrived. He was living in the desert doing reconnaissance on CVRTs for the brigade with the QDGs, he couldn't get out due to the flight restrictions. It was good to see him.

News started to filter through that the explosion wasn't IDF, it was an IED and that a casualty was being brought in. An order came through for all non-essential personnel to stay away from the med centre which was next to where I had signed for my vehicle. A 2 Mercian Officer, Captain Rupert William Michael Bowers had stood on an Old Italian anti-personnel mine which must have been planted next to the base with the sandstorm for cover. Captain Bowers was in the middle of the section which is unusual as it's normally the first man that gets hit. *"A soldier killed yesterday in an explosion in Afghanistan has been identified as a 24-year-old captain.*

Tributes have been paid to the 'bravest of the 'brave' Rupert Bowers who was killed by the blast from an improvised explosive device (IED) as he led a patrol in Helmand Province.

The married 24-year-old father, from Wolverhampton, had been working as a security adviser to the Afghan National Army.

He was part of the 2nd Battalion, The Mercian Regiment (Worcester's and Foresters), which was attached to 2nd Battalion The Rifles". (Daily Mail). This was Captain Bowers final patrol before leaving theatre. He was only 24. Molly and Suthers seen him come back in, everything from below the chest was missing. As the casualty evacuation helicopter came into extract Captain Bowers, 3 more whooshes but slower than the first salvo. The insurgents had waited for the angel's flight and aimed at the Pedro. They had used a system which mortar men in the British army use called bracketing. They watched there splashes and adjusted accordingly, they managed to hit the perimeter fence of the HLS (helicopter landing site).

It was clear that the insurgents were fully aware of what are tactics were. IDF, was always followed by a foot patrol, and a casualty was always followed by an air evacuation. The 2 Mercian lads were devastated, these lads were just about to cut out and this. They were at the side of the Mastiff in tears. I was gutted for them. There Troop leader came over a Lt Beetleman, his eyes were red raw and he could barely speak. He gathered his Troop together and spoke to them. He told them that crying was good and that it was okay to be in bits, it wouldn't be normal otherwise. I didn't know where to look and tried to move away but the lads said to stay, that it could happen to one of our lads in the coming months.

2 Fijian privates who were on the foot patrol, and were in shock jumped into the back of the Mastiff, I had just signed for. They had been on the stretcher to bring the body back, both looked lost. A RMP Staff Sergeant came down and asked to speak to them. Lt Beetleman closed the doors and said he would bring them back later, but just to give them some time. The RMP was becoming dismissive and was demanding to speak to them, his attitude was that now was the best time to speak to them and he had probably done more years in

the Army than Lt Beetleman had done months. Lt Beetleman stood his ground, I could see no value in interviewing them now, and to be honest the RMP should have left it. This is leadership.

It was around 1230, I had only had a few hours' sleep and my adrenaline was through the roof. I loaded my kit onto the Mastiff, strapping the Bergan to the front Armour and the day sack to the roof, via latch straps, which I didn't know how to use. Lt Beetleman was going to shadow me for a few days, showing me where the different bases and VPs were. There was an animosity between him and Mr McCullough, who he referred to as a stupid cunt, whereas Mr McCullough referred to him as reckless and indifferent. I could only assume that their paths had crossed at some point in Sandhurst or they had mutual friends or enemies, but they were both professional enough to crack on with the job.

My job was to be lead transport throughout the rip, I would take 1RWF guys from the main FOB, and swap them with 2 Mercian lads who were living along the 611 in smaller bases. Some were easy to get too, and others difficult. The problem with constantly being lead transport is that you have a choker/mine roller attached to the front of your vehicle which is an extension of around 1.5 meters, which you can't see any way as your that high up. Your vision from the Mastiff is difficult anyway and this makes driving twice as hard, you have to rely on your commander who is in the gunner's positions, who always fucking assumes you can see the same as him.

Throughout the day, I ripped guys out of every base in our area of operation, OP Tear, CP Langer, OP Salat, CP Baray (My Checkpoint) and CP Pankalay, where the other half of my troop where based. OP Tear was across a ridiculously small bridge at the bottom of the Kaker road. The Kaker road wasn't a road but a dirt track, which was barely able to take a Mastiff. It was in a small village surrounded by poppy crops. CP Langer wasn't much more accessible, why don't the engineers just work out the size width and weight of military wagons and build the bridges accordingly. As a driver it is all on you to get across these obstacles, and maintain the safety of the crew. OP Salat was a small base on the side of the 611, easily accessible, some of the RTR lads in my section were staying there. It was shared with the Afghan National Civil Order Police (ANCOP), who were a shower of scum. CP Baray where I ended up being based for most of my tour was actually quite comfortable, it had a large Tank Park, a multifunction gym with a rowing machine and a small cookhouse. The base was on a precipice and had 360 views of the surrounding areas. The ANCOP were based within a wider compound next to us, and were not allowed in our section armed. Finally CP Pankalay, which was 5km up the road from us, as our troop was split, 9 of our lads were based there, 3 crews. The problem with this base was that it was surrounded by hills, and it was 200 meters into the green zone, so you could not see a meter from your wall due to the overgrowth. Spotting a firing position from this point was insane. Also the ANCOP that were based there constantly set up vehicle checkpoints and robbed the locals of their produce, like some feudal taxation system. Due to this the base was getting hit daily by UGL.

Lt Beetleman sat beside me in the front of the wagon in the commander's chair which, was rarely used due to better visuals from the gunners mount. Much to Mr McCullough's annoyance I got on really well with Beets and we were having a laugh in the wagon. He told me of all the big incidents he had been involved in and that cameras had followed him for 6 months making a documentary. He told me he was driving up the road past VPs 4-5 when a mini bus swerved past them speeding, hit an off-road IED and killed 18, 5 children,

7 women and 6 men. He said his lads were shovelling up body parts and all needed trimmed. The Taliban also placed white flags out as shows of strength which had complex IEDs triggered underneath them. A women who had been working on a farm had triggered an IED close to a flag and had been killed, and he was in that much of a rage, he ordered the driver to take the flag down using the choker. But the IED blew the choker to bits and disabled the vehicle, so he was stuck there all night.

Beets explained that the daily routine was to do VP checks 1-9, these were vulnerable areas of the 611, culverts, bridges, broken tarmac and any area were you were forced to slow down, making you an easier target for snipers. He explained to me that a driver should get to know these places so that the commander just says VP2 and the driver goes straight there These were normally completed in the morning. Throughout the day a Mastiff crew would also be expected to do admin runs from FOB Ouellette. These consisted of dropping different kit out to the smaller locations, transportation of lads coming and going form R and R, VIP visits, shows of strength for the lads on foot patrol, moving detainees, and informers. The list was quite comprehensive but essentially any movement in the AO was completed in the Mastiffs. At night the Mastiff would go out and do counter IED, which was driving up and down the road with your lights off using infa-red night cameras for body heat. Another role came quite late on our tour which was force protection/ route domination which entailed driving up and down the road at night for 4 to 8 hours. Also the Mastiffs would sometimes act as targets in an OP Archer, as the Mastiffs were quite an easy target to aim for the insurgents liked firing at them. An OP Archer was a feign to draw insurgents, out, the Mastiff commander would then feed the firing point across the net and either air support or GLMRS (ground launched multiple rocket system) would wipe the grid out. I enjoyed doing these as on certain wagons we would all take turns on the top cover firing 200 rounds of link each. He explained that a rotation of crews was key and no crews should do more than 2 days at a time, as exhaustion could set in. Mr Beetleman I could see was a good young officer, he was 100% for his lads, and he put himself on the line in his ops room if he thought his Troop was getting treated unfairly.

I arrived in CP Baray around 2330, and everyone got out. I was shattered, a 2 Mercian Sgt then told me to jump back in the wagon and to run back down to Ouellette. It was just him and me in the wagon on our own and we headed away. British Army Standard Operating Procedures (SOPs) instruct that there has to be a minimum of 2 wagons out, in case one gets into trouble. This was just complacency, I said to him I wasn't comfortable, and he just said the lads are shattered, and in 6 months we haven't been hit once at night. We done a few of these runs across the AO that night, and when I got back I got 3 hours sleep and was back out again doing admin runs on the 611.

VP CHECKS 1-9

VP 1 was an enclosed firing point which was used to attack OP Salat. I was a simply a wall with a waist deep hole, that was not within camera range, how the Taliban knew this I never worked out. We would drive past this slowly with top cover inspecting it. VPs, 2, 3, 7 and 8 were all either culverts or bridges. We checked these by getting out of the vehicle and doing a series of counter IED drills. The reason they are VPs is an IED or command device can easily be planted there. VPs 4-5 were together. VP 4 was a hole in the road around 2 meters across and 6 inches deep, the Mastiff had to slow down to go over it, making it an easier target. VP 5 was underneath VP 4 it was a culvert, and this was easily the most dangerous one. VP 9 was an empty compound which overlooked Pan Kalay and was a known firing

point.

LIVING ACCOMADATION

There are several types of Base in theatre, the bigger

ones are called Camps such as Camp Bastion, where

rear Ops groups would be based, then FOBs, Forward

Operating Bases and MOBs Main Operating bases like

MOB Price and FOB Ouellette, large well protected

bases, CPs Checkpoints, smaller satellite stations which

you patrol from and Ops, Observation Posts, small

compound type bases which are used to observe a

particular vulnerable point.

TYPE 63 107MM SINGLE LAUNCHER

Chinese rocket system also manufactured in Iran.

Airburst are likely to be a malfunction as proxy fuses

are rare. The rockets may be used in conjunction with

rudimentary, make shift launch tubes and rails or in a

direct role.

24/03/2012 DAY FOUR

Mr McCullough had sent Molly and the only other driver in our multiple who could drive the choker Suthers to OP Salat on our first day. This was a fucking stupid decision that made no sense what so ever, 2 Welsh NCOs shared the driving of the second Mastiff, were I was left all week to drive the lead. I was exhausted, the longest unbroken sleep I got all week was just over 3 hours and this was on the wagon parked outside CP Langer. My body was hanging. The other RTR lads had still not left Bastian as the 1RWF were prioritising there lads for flights. I couldn't wait until they got here as Gwilliam and Minty were both driver trained. The Boss was a nightmare and I was quickly losing patience with him. Des and I were the only other RTR lads in CP Baray as Des couldn't drive and wasn't needed as a gunner he just sat off on the camp all day, I don't understand why he wasn't swapped with Suthers as OP Salat was an observation post which you didn't patrol from.

Des wasn't getting it easy either, as the Welsh were falling into CP routine, shorts, flip flops, the boss made Des and I walk around fully kitted up carrying our helmets, rifles and body armour. I told him that we looked like complete lunatics and that the Welsh were laughing at us, but he didn't care, he said that this would be a RTR thing. Mr McCullough was constantly clashing with the 1RWF Sgt. Sgt Dean had just been promoted and had just came from an infantry phase 1 training establishment and made everyone including the Officers and the NCOs he had known for years call him by rank.

He clearly wanted Mr McCullough out of the CP and seen me as a way of doing it. Two welsh NCOs spoke to me and said they would support me in a complaint against Mr McCullough, to get him moved either to OP

Salat permanently or an Ops room role in FOB Ouellette. I said I would speak to him and try and get him to calm down and take a step back. This had Sgt Dean written all over it, because I couldn't stand him he wouldn't ask me directly. Sgt Dean and Mr McCullough's relationship was deteriorating rapidly and was spilling out into open arguments within the CP. I would always back Mr McCullough over any of the Welsh but it was hard to jump to his defence when he made silly mistakes. It was clearly us and them, only there was about 40 of them and 3 of us. Craig and Mr McCullough had told us that we wouldn't be classed as attachments by the Welsh and we would be treated as part of their Reg. The first thing the Welsh put up in the CP was there Regimental Cap badge with all their names and our names in small writing underneath as an attached arm. I could have fucking strangled Craig over this with all the shit I put up with in pre-deployment training how we were all one.

The command structure in CP Baray weren't including him in briefings or telling him what was going on, I was fuming over this as Mr McCullough was finding it difficult. I was being briefed independently as Sgt Dean and Mr Hoare were both being used to command the lead wagon. Word came across the net that the RTR lads were flying into FOB Ouellette that afternoon, so we arranged to have lunch there and meet them. As there flight made an attempt to land the insurgents fired 3 rockets at it, it was mental watching a merlin do evasive manoeuvres in the air.

I collared Macca and explained to him what had been happening and as the senior guy he had to talk to the Boss. Macca was only a Lance jack, but he said he would do it, but that the Boss would know that it had came from me as he had only just arrived. One of the lads who had got off the flight was Tucker and he had lost his daysack with all his ammunition in it and bedding. This was his first fucking day on the ground and nobody was in the mood for this sort of fuck up. This turned into a merry go round, with all the RTR lads looking for his kit throughout the FOB. Admin is a personal job and you should be on top of it. His daysack turned up on the HLS site as he had left it at his ass.

We went back to CP Baray and immediately got bugged out to go to OP Tir, Sgt Dean wanted to take the rear vehicle as lead, which was not equipped with a mine roller. I told him that I wouldn't be doing that and he started screaming at me, I said the whole purpose of a mine roller was to go to the front and activate pressure plate IEDs, he was way out of line and I wasn't for backing down as this is a straight SOP (standard operating procedure) which saves lives. Macca got on to it as well and backed me up. Sgt Dean wasn't prepared to lose face in front of his men and said that the RTR weren't needed or wanted on camp, he looked foolish saying that as none of his men could fully crew the wagons. Mr McCullough came over to see what was happening but Sgt Dean just fucked him off.

Macca said to me come on let them crew them and we walked back to our accommodation which was a camp bed under hard cover. 2 minutes later Cpl Warren (Waz) came into the hard cover and asked me to take the lead wagon with Sgt Dean as commander to OP tear as no one else was confident to take the choker over the bridge and across the dirt track. This was humble pie and beyond pathetic. Macca came with me as a familiarisation patrol with Sgt Dean as top cover. He had toned down and was very positive about my driving and was asking questions about home. Sometimes tempers flare when your under pressure, but professionalism should always come first, plus he would have been fucked if I had have went man down as they would have been stuck in CP Baray.

When we got to the village which OP Tir was in the atmospherics quickly changed and I know it's a cheesy saying and a stinking shout but you could feel the tension. All the villagers were shouting their kids in and taking their livestock into their homes. Afghans are used to seeing AFVs and kids always ask the troops for sweets. An ISTAR (intelligence, surveillance, target, accusation, reconnaissance), operator came across the net and informed Sgt Dean that a blue Toyota pick-up had been tailing us and stopped on the track we had used and was suspected of planting an IED. Sgt Dean directed me to bomb across the desert and use any alternative route, we had a laugh testing the limitations of the Mastiff across sand and I lost my first set of back steps on this day. We went back into FOB Ouellette and we heard a small explosion, the Brigade QRF (quick reaction force), went out to investigate. The intelligence we had received was correct the pickup did plant an IED, but a six year old Afghan boy had set it off and was killed. We went past the point again and it was covered in blood and body parts.

When we got to or CP Macca spoke to Mr McCullough, I wasn't present but I think he told him just to take a step back and to get off the lads case. Mr McCullough knew it was down to me that he had been criticized. After that he wasn't expecting us to walk around kitted up with our rifles. I was on a brief that night and almost our full section was there. 2 other fully trained drivers had arrived that day, Minty and Gwilliam. I was looking forward to a bit of a break, but Sgt Dean put Gwilliam on camp guard and Minty was put as a gunner. I spoke to the Boss about this saying it was fucking non-sense and that Minty, Gwilliam and Suthers had basically had a week off, when I was getting thrashed. He said that it was Sgt Deans decision and he was unwilling to discuss it with him due to his confrontational nature. I told him that he had pips on his chest and that Sgt Dean had stripes, but he walked away.

97

I spoke to Sgt Dean and said that this was a fucking joke, but he said this wasn't done to antagonise me, he said he would be putting the other RTR lads in the second wagon, following me as I knew the AO. When they were as comfortable as me he would then change it. I could see the pragmatic approach in his argument, and he said that he would remove me from the STAG rotation. I had done a week of twenty hour days and he was asking me to do this for another week, with the back wagon alternating drivers. Effectively what had been taking place were full crew rotations of both wagons, bar me who just stayed constant in the lead.

26/03/2012 DAY SIX

The ANSF had made good on their promise and shot 2 British soldiers just south of our AO. Sgt Luke Taylor, of the Royal Marines, and L/Cpl Michael Foley were shot when they turned their backs on an Afghan National Security soldier in a Sanger in a HQ in Lashkar

Gah in Helmand province, southern Afghanistan. *"It is with sadness that the Ministry of Defence must confirm that Sergeant Luke Taylor, of the Royal Marines, and Lance Corporal Michael Foley, of the Adjutant General's Corps (Staff and Personnel Support), were killed in Afghanistan on Monday, 26 March 2012." (UK Forces in Afghanistan, WordPress).*

28/03/2012 DAY EIGHT

I got told to pack up a day sack for 3 nights and that I was going on a Mastiff 3 course in Camp Bastion, as I had been picked to work with the ANSF Tiger Teams. The ANSF Tiger Teams are the ANSFs special forces and ISAF wanted them to start raiding compounds and running VCPs. As ISAF (International Security Assistance Force) Troops were not allowed into villages it would be easier to send them in. The problem with this was that the Tiger Teams were trigger happy cowboys whose weapon drills were really poor. A

Fusilier called Gibbo and an RTR trooper called Brown were going with me.

Brown was from the other multiple and I got on really well with him. I had met Gibbo in training and he was a good lad, he was involved in an accident on one of the ranges in training, where he fired a shot which went through a barricade and killed another Fusilier. I didn't mention it to him as I didn't know him well enough to discuss it, but this must have affected him. I went to the gym in Fob Ouellette that day and met SM Mills, we chatted about how things were going and the possible problems they were facing with manpower when R and R kicked in. R and R starts when you are 6 weeks into tour and ends when you have 6 weeks left. There is a 3 month window, for all the lads to get 2 weeks R and R in.

The main topic or talking point regardless of rank in a FOB, CP, OP, is when is you're R and R? Rest and

Relaxation is a 14 day point throughout your tour where you get to fly back to the UK. Ideally you want your R and R dates at the half way point or as late as possible so you can front load your tour and have less to do when you arrive back. The dates are picked before you start tour, and you go into a pool and bid for certain dates. SM Mills explained they wouldn't be able to carry out an effective role in the AO due to the numbers going down I had a lot of time and respect for the SM but I couldn't help thinking did they not fucking realise this beforehand and account for it. I used the internet had a decent meal, a good shower and shave and watched 2 films in the welfare tent, Crocodile Dundee and the Naked Gun 2.

I attended a memorial service in FOB Ouellette at dusk in front of the cross and mount. There was another gold plaque on it. The service was for Captain Bowers, Sgt Taylor and L/Cpl Foley, "When you go home tell them of us and say: for your tomorrow we gave our today", this is from the famous epitaph in the Kohima allied War cemetery in Burma. The memorial service took place by candle light and the Welsh RSM said "we will remember them" and the last post was played, as the flags were brought down to half-mast.

At 0230 I went up to the HLS, I had never been on a helicopter before, so was excited. We boarded really quickly and you can feel the heat of the engines. Because the Taliban in our AO loved firing rockets at the Helicopters the rotors were always turning and only landed for a matter of seconds. The next thing I remember was Gibbo shaking me awake as we landed in Bastion. For some reason Gibbo had about six bowman radios and several boxes which me and Brown helped him off the helicopter with. We were met by a 1RWF MT creature who ran us to a transit tent.

In the morning we went for breakfast, then down to the RSOI compound to do the Mastiff 3 training. It was a

Lance Jack from D SQN, who just signed our FMTs, so I went for a haircut, and then to the gym. The difference between Bastion and a CP are insane. The people who work in Bastian get the same wage as a grunt on the ground. They live in air conditioned rooms and have pods for beds. They eat in cookhouses which are like 4 star restaurants, and the gym facilities are better than David Lloyd. Bastion has shops, KFC, Pizza Hut, coffee shops and top class welfare facilities. If anyone ever said they went on tour then add that they were based in Bastion, I instantly lose respect for them.

We arranged to meet for coffee and go to Pizza Hut later that night. Brown was constantly on the phone and using the internet, I asked him if everything was okay, but he just said he was missing home, and his Mrs was stressing him out. He had forgot his head dress, and every remf with rank in Bastion was gripping him for it, but he was just running away, which was hysterical. A few days in Bastion was just what I needed, I had been on worse holidays.

31/03/2012 DAY ELEVEN/ GUARD

I was back in CP Baray after a relaxing 3 days in Bastion. I arrived around 1200, so was put on CP Guard. CP Guard is where you have time off patrols, you do jobs in the camp which the people who are on patrols don't have time to do. The jobs are basic CP tidiness, burning rubbish, shit bags, cooking food and doing Dixie's, which are the pots used for cooking. It was a break from the relentless patrolling, and was a lot safer as the CP was heavily protected. In my absence a rota had been drawn up for patrols, guard and the manning of OP Salat which Mr Hoare's 1 platoon had to look after. Everybody in 1 platoon would do a 20 day rotation in CP Baray, where the main role was patrols and CP guard, and a 10 day stint in OP Salat, which being an Observation post you didn't have to patrol from or carry out any of the admin tasking's, across the AO. So effectively you worked for twenty days in CP Baray then relaxed for 10 days in OP Salat. The only people who were not on this rotation were Suthers, Gwilliam and Me, as we were drivers there were also 3 other drivers which the Welsh refused to use. Also when in CP Baray you were 3 days on then 3 days off, but the drivers were 6 days on patrols and 3 days on CP guard. Which didn't make sense if someone was on R and R or went man down due to illness. Every other 1RTR commander and gunner were on this rotation. I spoke to Mr McCullough about this, saying to include other drivers within the rotation and to be treated equally in the CP. I was unhappy that he had allowed this blatant and outright unfair system take place, as the highest rank in the CP. He had no answers, only to say that he acknowledged that it was wrong but was unwilling to approach the 1 Platoon hierarchy about it as he was worried it would end in a confrontation.

I went and spoke to Mr Hoare the 1 platoon troop leader, he was young around 24 and from the south west. He explained to me that due to the amount of IEDs and instances of small arms fire in the AO that it looked like it would go the same way as the 2 Mercian's and that all foot-patrols would be cancelled. He said that we would revert back to our main objective which was maintaining the security of the 611 and keeping it open. Mr Hoare also explained to me that neither he nor Sgt Dean would be taking the easy option of OP Salat and that between them they would be doing 3 days on CP guard and 3 days on patrols, and that when they were on R and R Cpl Warren would slot in to their role. He said everything that we would be doing for the foreseeable future would be based around a fully operational Mastiff. The 2 lads he had, could drive the rear Mastiff, but both were not fully confident on maintenance. One of the lads didn't realise the fan belt had snapped and ran the oil and coolant out destroying the engine. This involved a platoon size recovery, and kept them off the road for 30 hours.

Molly and Suthers had been replaced in OP Salat by Macca and Des. Molly simply wasn't getting on with Mr McCullough and was siding with the Welsh, havening his dinner with them and going for a smoke with them. I said that as the next highest 1 RTR rank he needed to start supporting him, and stop isolating him. Molly pointed out the difficulties that I was having, and I told him that I kept my disagreements one on one, and only discussed any issues with other RTR lads. Molly was openly derogatory concerning the Boss and was agreeing more and more with the Welsh rank. Molly said he would try, but that Mr McCullough had to stop interfering with the way the CP was run. That's when I knew Molly had firmly threw his hat in with the Welsh.

OP SALAT

OP Salat was a small Observation Post on the 611 which houses both ISAF and ANSF Troops. It had the record for being the most contacted base in the history of the Herrick's. This was due to its proximity to Kunjack Hill. Just to the west of Kunjack Hill were two small transient poppy farmers' villages, imaginably named Taliban Town 1 and Taliban Town 2. The Taliban policed these towns and ran all the poppy across the AO. Kunjack Hill had several compounds and vegetation growths which were perfect firing points to hit OP Salat. There was also a track perfect for scramblers to get in and out of.

APRIL

"A soldier will fight long and hard for a bit of colored ribbon."

Napoleon Bonaparte

01/04/2012DAY TWELVE/ REME

As a driver you are responsible for the wagon. You have to make sure all your personal kit is in order the exact same as the infantry, then you have to make sure all the vehicle maintenance is complete. With a Mastiff you have to do a pre-use check, at least once a day. These consist of a levels check, oil, diesel, coolant, brake fluid, water, transmission oil, and check all the pressures tyre, oil, an integrity check of the Hull, armour. You also have to make sure the wagon is kitted out with ample rations and water, also maintaining the cleanliness of the interior. This is on top of doing the after use checks. On top of this you have multiple document which need to be filled in daily, driver's hours, pre and post use checks. Due to the 1RTR gunners Minty, Bob and Des, simply not looking after the weapons the drivers were also responsible for cleaning the weapon system and ammunition supply.

Today we had to go to FOB Ouellette to do a 3 monthly maintenance check on the wagon I had signed for 12 days ago. The drivers completed a series of checks, supervised by the REME. The commanders and Barmead teams which were in the back, viewed these days as effectively days off. They would all go and use the welfare facilities in the FOB, phone, internet, shower, gym, proper meals. The driver however had to stay with the vehicle to complete the Checks. A Mastiff is accessed through the back, with the drivers chair at the front. When we stopped somewhere with welfare facilities a driver couldn't use them due to being the last person off the wagon, all the facilities would be used by the passengers and commanders.

The REME in Fob Ouellette were some of the hardest working people I met out there. The job they had was relentless, 0700-0200 were not uncommon hours for the REME to work. I became friends with a full screw called Chris Lunn from Sheffield, he was basically running the REME in the FOB. Chris hated seeing us, as it always involved some complex job which we as drivers couldn't do. I spent hours with the REME covered in oil, underneath wagons. The REME were like tankies they just cracked on until the job was done. If they didn't have the parts they would just cannibalise another vehicle which was damaged. Getting parts in CF Burma was impossible as the flights were restricted, so we had to normally drive to the next base in Lash as helicopters could land there.

03/04/2012 DAY FOURTEEN/ CONTACT

Pan Kalay exploded today and the other section in our Troop got really busy. Every day they had been coming under some level of IDF and sniper fire. For some reason however they were still operating foot patrols from the front gate of the CP. The 2 Mercian's didn't do this due to Pan Kalay being in the green zone and the level of threat being so high. One of the 1RWF TA attachments got shot in the hip, I didn't know him but he was called pudding. Molly and I jumped in the Mastiff and along with Sgt Dean blocked off a section of the 611 to get him cas evaced out. I could hear Craig over the net giving grids, and seen Jay and Mo running on a stretcher with a big fat bloke on it. There were constant cracks of gunfire and flashes of flame. Then a MERT (Medical emergency response team), in what looked like a Black Hawk (*the* Black Hawk helicopter *series can perform a wide array of missions, including the tactical transport of troops, electronic warfare, and aeromedical evacuation*) landed on the tarmac of the 611, Craig had set smoke off everywhere and it looked like a scene from a movie. Jay had celloxed the wound and there was blood all over him. Mo then jumped on the 50 and then started to provide cover fire for the extraction.

Just as we were bugging out, Mr Hoare came over the net with a contact report. The section he was on foot patrol with came under fire around 2km from our CP. They were on a ridge line taking sniper fire from the green zone and needed Armour. We went across difficult terrain which had never had anything other than a horse and cart on it and got to the lads in about 15 minutes. The section was sweating out. When bullets are fired you feel what is like a whip over your head were the air is dispersed if it's close. Due to all the noise in the AO Mr Hoare, couldn't work out a firing point, so the lads were just firing into the desert.

04/04/2012 DAY FIFTEEN/ STUCK

We got roped into a waste of time partnering role today, with the Americans and Ancop, south of our AO. We were just to follow a convey of MRAPs (Mine-Resistant Ambush Protected), War Hammer (American IED patrol), ANCOP Hum Vs, attach ourselves onto the end it couldn't be easier. I think the purpose was a show of strength around a Taliban village which we couldn't patrol in. It was also the first time I had been in a complete crew, Mr McCullough was commanding. Minty on the gun and I was driving. This was Minty's first patrol and Mr McCullough's first time as lead vehicle. Sgt Dean was in the 2nd wagon with Gwilliam driving. I had been out almost every day and I was fairly confident with the capabilities of the Mastiff, Mr McCullough and Minty had been marking time in the CP.

I was surprised Sgt Dean had let Mr McCullough go in the lead as he always went first. We went to our meeting point and allowed the convey to go ahead of us. It was made up of a lot of wagons, a huge amount of firepower. There was also air support hovering around. They went up a dirt track at around 10km per hour. The lead wagon was fitted with a mine roller. Instead of us following the proven route which had around 400 tons of armour on it the Boss decides to use the desert next to the track. I explained that I didn't think that the sand would hold a 30 ton Mastiff, but he was insistent. Minty agreed with me. The Boss said we were being tactical and would use a different route. We immediately got stuck. The choker went in and the front wheels just embedded themselves. The American's couldn't wait so they carried on, while Sgt Deans wagon pulled us out.

The Boss was ashen faced and tried to put a positive spin on it, that it was some type of learning curve. I went into sulking child mode. Even though this was not my fault, my competence would be called into question as it was obvious that the sand would not take the weight. What he didn't get was that no one would say anything to him, but I would be the butt of jokes. I explained to him that when I was unsure of something out here I always took the cautious option, he agreed and said he would take on-board advice in future.

117

We just set off again to try and catch up with the convey, when Minty started to scream. He had got his hand stuck in the turret traverse and ripped the skin off his wee finger through a set of Oakley gloves. I stopped to investigate but Mr McCullough wanted me to crack on. I stopped any way and jumped in the back. A medic was in the back and started to patch Minty up, but it just wouldn't stop bleeding. A fusilier called Coy jumped on the gun. I spoke to Mr McCullough and said that we should radio it through and go back to FOB Ouellette, the medic agreed with me but the Boss wouldn't do it. We carried on for four hours with Minty in the back with a minor crush injury.

When we got to the med centre in the FOB, his hand was that bad a PEDRO was called to take him back to Bastion, and OP Minimise came over the net. This was a bad decision by Mr McCullough the priority should always be the lads. When we got back to our CP Sgt Dean was raging and gripped me straight away. I thought he was going to pull me apart, but he just asked

what was going on in the wagon. He was surprised I got

stuck and asked me why I went that way. He was also

raging about Minty. I didn't have much to do with Sgt

Dean in the CP so it was unusual for us to talk. He

didn't want the Boss in the front wagon and he didn't

want Minty in the CP. He told me that if anything like

this happened again I would be given extra duties in the

CP. I just accepted it. Even though this was 100% Mr

McCullough's fault and as the senior rank he should

have took responsibility.

12/04/2012 DAY TWENTY/ DOUBLE IED STRIKE

We were on QRF (quick reaction force), based in our

CP. QRF means that when something happens in the

AO, you are the call sign which goes out to investigate

it. Being on QRF is very much a mixed bag, you could

have the whole day to yourself, sunbathing, reading or

working out, or you could be 40 hours on a cordon

waiting on Brimstone (Bomb disposal). This day was the latter. Jay Walker had been running a transport to a new CP called CP Berkshire. His Mastiff had hit a massive IED blowing the front of his vehicle up and destroying his choker. The problem was CP Berkshire was in the middle of the Desert and could only be accessed by tracked vehicles, so why Jay was going there in a Mastiff convoy we couldn't work out.

Our job was to provide cover for the REME SVR (support vehicle recovery) which would recover Jay. I ended up in the rear wagon with Molly and Mr McCullough went in the front. When we got down to Jay, there was bits of his wagon everywhere and a large crater. There were also rows of stones and IED indicators everywhere. In pre-deployment training you are told of the IED threat. IEDs are triggered by various methods, including remote control, infra-red or magnetic triggers, pressure-sensitive bars or trip wires (victim-operated). In some cases, multiple IEDs are wired together in a daisy-chain, to attack a convoy of vehicles spread out along a roadway. There are 4 main types. The most common is a pressure plate IED. You effectively push 2 plates together with the weight of your vehicle or foot, this completes a circuit which initiates a charge, which then ignites explosives, very simple to make and very effective. These can be planted and left by insurgents on known ISAF routes. That is why we try not to set patterns. The insurgents leave signs, or IED indicators so that the local population don't trigger them accidently. Jay had missed all these signs. Other IEDs are RC (radio controlled), these are set off by a remote signal, such as a mobile phone or antenna. The ECM we have with us neutralises this type of device so it is rare that ISAF get targeted with it. Another is Command wire were a charge is sent to the device as you are passing, and command pull where a switch is pulled by an insurgent at distance which initiates the device. The list however is endless.

121

Mr McCullough's wagon was hit by a smaller charge on the approach to Jay's wagon which blew his front wheel up, it didn't disable the wagon as the choker took the weight. This was 2 mobility kills which cost around £100,000 in manpower and vehicles, whereas the IEDs would have cost around £10. It was too dangerous to bring Brimstone out at night so we decided to STAG on until first light. There were no rations on the wagon due to the Welsh camp NCO, a little fat Hitler refusing to give them too me. There were 2 welsh full screws in the back, who explained to me this wouldn't happen again. I just went to sleep and rotated on the gun. I could have been a knob head and pulled drivers hours as some people did, but I would never do that to the lads. As Mr McCullough was senior rank on the other wagon, he made the lads sleep in their body armour, which is just fucking mental.

Brimstone (*The Counter IED Task Force is made up of a number of small teams, code name Brimstone, that include bomb disposal operators and the searchers who look for IEDs in the most dangerous areas*)   said they would come at first light, and I believed them as this was the first time I had dealt with them. First light in Afghanistan is normally about 0430, the locals are up for prayers around that time and the farm workers start to go to work. Breakfast time in FOB Ouellette is at 0630 to 0800. Instead of arriving at first light Brimstone waited until breakfast then came down, this was a stunt they pulled the entire time we were there.

Brimstone proved a route and we went back to FOB Ouellette. We had just been in the vehicle for 20 hours, and we got an immediate tasking to do VPs 1-9. The clueless 1RWF 2ic, who worked in the ops room hadn't a clue.

14/04/2012 DAY TWENTY TWO/ SRR

It was a Saturday, not that this mattered on Tour but for 3 Mondays in a row on VPs 4-5 wed found DFCs (directional fragmentation charges), it's basically an improvised claymore. They'll take a metal tube, pack it with explosives, and they'll pack shrapnel in front of that. We had a Special Reconnaissance regiment (SRR) team come up from Bastion to plant cameras and watch the position. SRR are a Special Forces branch of the tri-services, and are a mixture of different regiments.

Their Sgt explained to me that they would plant motion sensors cameras, and remotely detonated claymores at the DFC point. If the Taliban planted anything they could be easily targeted. I was really impressed at first. Then we done a number of recce runs past the point, and basically saturated the area. I took a team in and drooped them off at 2300 and arranged to be back at 0430, I was also put on ops runner at 0200-0300 which I was unhappy about. A 1RWF Lance jack was continually writing an unfair stag list for ops room runner. The Welsh outnumbered us by around 30 lads on camp, but the RTR lads were getting 0100-0500. I spoke to Mr McCullough about it and he just shrugged. As a driver you are meant to have at least 6 hours unbroken sleep in 24. This isn't real on tour and the best you can hope for is around 4. I went and spoke to the Welsh NCO a L/Cpl Nurse and explained that I would take the last 5 STAG lists to the 1RWF SM in FOB Ouellette and get him to speak to Sgt Dean. The list was changed, and other NCOs did it instead of him. When Crouchy or Waz did a stag list it was always fair. Both knew I liked running in the morning so would put me on an hour before reveille so I could get a run in first thing.

I was with SRR for the next few days just doing admin runs and movements. Nothing was planted over the weekend and I had to go with them to remove the equipment. This was on top of counter IED, VP checks and route domination

17/04/2012 DAY TWENTY FIVE/ D & V

Mr McCullough went man down today with D & V. Diarrhoea and Vomiting bug is very common on tour and is brought about by poor hygiene. It can rapidly spread, so if you have it you are isolated due to the contagious nature. It absolutely debilitates you, and you can take only fluids. The only cure is rest, normally 48 hours. This was the start of twenty days of people going man down with D and V. the medic Mason's head was wrecked. The reality of the epidemic that rocked the camp, was that the lads were tired. When they seen one person get a few days off, they just copied them. I didn't have one day off or miss a patrol due to sickness, I washed before meals and followed the training guidelines to prevent it. There were lads in the CP that had 5 instances of D and V throughout the tour. It was non-sense as your body's natural defences built up. This got to me as if someone didn't want to go out this was the first excuse they used. It was so fucking weak. I didn't trust the cooking in the CP and could not be annoyed fighting with the Welsh over ration boxes, so just ate the food that Sharon sent me in welfare boxes. She had sent so many in the first two months I had no room to store them and had to ask her to stop sending them. Also Crouchys Mum worked for an Armed Forces charity so she sent us out hundreds.

18/04/2012 DAY TWENTY SIX/ INTEL

We received intelligence today that insurgents were coming into the AO from Pakistan and were planning a Tet Offensive after the poppy harvest. On the 25th it was Mujahedeen day. This was the day the Soviets were beaten out of Afghanistan by Muslim fighters, trained by the British and armed by the Americans. Several of these fighters joined the Taliban or went to fight Jihad in other Muslim conflicts.

21/04/2012 DAY TWENTY SIX/ DETAINEE

So far things were just feeling like one long day, and I was constantly exhausted. I was struggling to get into any form of routine due to the way I was being used. Everything was based around the Mastiff, the platoon were simply redundant without me, it sounds big headed but it was reality. Because of our proximity to the green zone the land around us was fertile. Everywhere, even right up to the gates of the CP were covered in poppy. Poppy is the plant heroin is derived from and Afghanistan is one of the biggest distributors

We had intelligence that the Taliban were waiting for the harvest and then they would attack us. So far we had just been finding a lot of IEDs and getting short bursts of small arms fire. The Terps, (interpreters), had been hearing a lot of different dialects on their iccom scanners, and there was rumours jihadists form Bosnia, Chechnya, Somalia, Iraq and Pakistan were coming into the AO. The Terps were horrible and untrustworthy, and I distanced myself from them. Once they couldn't understand a heavily accented insurgent on the iccom and when the Army interpreters listened the accent was from the midlands.

The 1RTR lads were also authorised to go on foot patrol due to the inability of the 1RWF to man the tour. I think out of all the RTR lads that went, only Macca, Molly and I actually went on the ground successfully. I was unhappy about this, as it was just another job role on top of everything else I was doing. My opinion of Craig changed as well. When he was told his lads would be going out he said no. He knew that we would just be used to carry kit and he refused to accept it. He said he wasn't prepared to put any of his section at a risk they simply weren't trained for and that his job was to protect the lads. Mr McCullough on the other hand said nothing, and made sure that he didn't go out.

At a VCP (vehicle checkpoint) in Pan Kalay they detained a high value target. A man was detained after coming up as positive on a HIDE camera. His DNA had been found at the site of several IED blasts. There was also a rumour that he was responsible for planting the IED which killed the 6 soldiers in the warrior before tour. Molly and I picked him up in the Mastiff and escorted him down to the RMP office in FOB Ouellette. He was kicking off in the wagon, threatening us all. Molly was telling everyone that we had caught him, but that wasn't the case it was 2 platoon.

23/04/2012 DAY TWENTY EIGHT/ FRICTION

The Boss had went to OP Salat for 10 days and Molly was left to run the troop. Molly took the front wagon and I was on the rear one with Macca. Driving the rear one was like having a day off, you had no choker, and you weren't constantly checking ground sign as the lead was proving the route. We were doing admin runs, which consisted of dropping ECM parts across the AO, VPs and route domination. Macca and Molly simply did not work well together and always tried to get one up on the other. We had been up for around 18 hours doing runs and we got tasked to go to OP Tear. Op Tear is always getting hit so you have to be really careful and the route is a nightmare. On the way back Molly went the wrong way down a track which a Mastiff couldn't make. Molly had been in OP Salat a lot and wasn't that sure of the AO. I spoke to Macca and he told Molly, "my driver said you're going the wrong way, reverse back and reroute". This was plain and simple English and good voice procedure, as it covered the mistake. Molly for a reason I will never understand came back saying he knew where he was going and stated "out". I told Macca he was going to get stuck, but Macca refused to go on the net again. The ground was far too lose and sandy like a beech and I was refusing to drive down it, but Macca told me to follow on at a distance. Molly got stuck and almost tipped the wagon. The Mastiff was on its passenger side wheels and the bar armour was preventing it from falling on its side. We

131

had to call for the SVR and the QRF to come to rescue him, as we couldn't self-recover.

Also the ground had to be proved for IEDs so the infantry in the back had to get out and go into their drills. It was a nightmare. I was fuming this was easily prevented, I blamed Molly and Macca. We turned a 30 min admin run into an 8 hour 50 man rescue operation. Macca loved seeing Molly fuck up. When we got back to the CP Molly asked us not to report it, and he would put it down as a road collapse. I had been covering up for the Boss for around a month so I said okay, but anything like that again, I would be speaking to Jay.

We got a few hours' sleep and were out again, we had been working for around 40 hours. We were up and down the 611, Molly was flying in the wagon and the driver Gwilliam wasn't used to the choker and was all over the road. Sgt Dean had went out to do a night patrol, and we were picking him up soon. We were struggling to keep up with Molly's wagon when he went into CP Baray, there was a wire across the ground which was barb wire. A fusilier got out to move it, from Molly's wagon and he drove into the CP without him. This was crazy, leaving a soldier alone on the 611 was just insane, I picked him up in my wagon and drove in after him. To enter the CP you had to go across a long narrow bridge made out of dirt, Molly's wagon had threw the choker over it and he had almost fell of the bridge, when we got there he was trying to self-recover. I spoke to Macca and said this was unacceptable. We entered the CP and Molly jumped out of the wagon and started screaming at us, I ignored him, and asked the other 2 crew members what was happening on the fucking wagon. Bob and Gwilliam refused to say anything as Molly had briefed them to be silent. They both came to see me after and said that Molly was telling Gwilliam to hurry and was making them rush their drills.

Molly was a full screw and I was only a trooper, so he pulled rank on me, saying he was in charge of the troop and would do whatever he wanted, and he would report me to Sgt Dean for questioning rank. Macca didn't back me as questioning rank is a big no no on tour.

We ended up in FOB Ouellette later on that day after doing an overnight IED cordon on the 611 and I ran into Jay walker. Jay was the same rank as Molly but was the troop corporal. I told him Molly needed spoken to, but I didn't go into specific detail, but Jay said Macca and the Boss had both had concerns. What I didn't know is that Macca had seen Jay before me and fucking slated Molly, but had asked Jay not to say he had said anything. I told Jay to tell Molly that I wanted him spoke to. Jay was sound, I told him that Macca and Molly were destroying the troop and that the Boss was becoming increasingly more isolated by the Welsh in the CP. I said he would have to see Craig and approach the Boss and ask him to take a step back. Because Mr

McCullough wasn't part of the CP command structure, he was torturing the crews of the Mastiffs he was commanding. He was in authority overload, micro-managing every aspect of my driving and the gunner's role. We were rotating crews through him, so as to give the lads a break on the wagon. The guy just wasn't learning, he kept trying to win the respect of the 1RWF, were I was just blanking them. Jay said that it was difficult to talk to the Boss as he wouldn't admit that anything was wrong.

26/04/2012 DAY THIRTY ONE/ ND

We were on QRF in the CP and we got bugged out to pick up a casualty in CP Pan Kalay. Sgt Dean was in the front wagon, and I was in the rear with Macca. I didn't see who was put into the front mastiff but it was ISAF and he was on a stretcher. When we got to the HLS in FOB Ouellette, we seen Trooper Brown from our troop be taken out, his leg was bandaged. Macca and I just thought that he was hit by sniper fire, but it ended up he had a ND (negligent discharge) in the Sanger with a pistol. He was taken by MERT and that was the last we seen of him. Craig and Jay were in the FOB and he gathered us together to speak to him. I felt for Craig, there was no way you can anticipate anything like this happening. The guy was stunned. Even though it was Brown who had shot himself, it would reflect badly on hum. We had all been trained on how to use pistols and are drills were up to date. It didn't make any sense. During training there was a clique of young ones in the troop who just messed about, making beeping noises, silly sounds and talking during lessons. Brown, Tucker, Sansom and Macca were always getting shouted at. Brown and Tucker were the worst though and they should have been taken off the tour, but the options to replace them were slim.

The 1RWF soldiers made fun of us non-stop after this and it was thrown in our faces during every argument over the next five months. We were called shit soldiers and this incident was always used as an example. After this the 1RTR lads were banned from using pistols. Brown had shot himself on the 31 day of tour. This date is significant, because if you are on the ground for more than 30 days and get injured you are entitled to a full tour bonus and all your tour pay, including a medal.

Jay had spoken to Molly and told him that if there was any more complaints from the section that paperwork and charges would be processed against him, he had told him that I had spoken to him, but that Macca had slated him. Jay was switched on enough to see Maccas game. He knew they hated each other and that Macca was trying to make me look like I had grassed. Molly asked to speak to me back at our CP, his whole attitude had changed and he was being sound. I told him that I don't report people lightly and that I tried to speak to him four times and he just ignored me. I explained to him that he was now viewed as one of the Welsh in camp and that this would come back to haunt him. He admitted he was out of order over not listening but said he was really struggling to work with Mr McCullough. I said to him that Craig, Jay and Macca had all went for him over trying to cover stuff up and it had to fucking stop. I told him that Mr McCullough would play a long game, ride out the next few months, and then get Molly back when it came to report time. I also told him that if I tried to speak to him one more time with any concerns I would ignore the chain of command and speak to Capt Rooney the welfare officer at our RHQ (regimental headquarters). Molly knew without doubt I would do this and he said he would listen anytime. We shook hands and that the end of it.

MAY

"In a man-to-man fight, the winner is he who has one more round in his magazine."

Erwin Rommel

01/05/2012 DAY THIRTY SIX/ R AND R

Minty was back from Bastion and we were operating as a complete crew again. The last few days had went without incident. Minty and the Boss clashed a lot on the wagon, as Minty was a trained commander. The Boss got annoyed when Minty was on top cover as he would talk directly to me, I always played on this pretending to make mistakes calling Minty, Boss or Sir, which increased the tension between them.

A hammer blow hit 11 troop that day, the 1RWF changed almost everyone in our troops R and R dates bringing them forward as their 2ic, didn't process the dates correctly before we left. This devastated the morale of our troop. I was simply the mighty oak and said I wouldn't be fucking bamboo   , change my fucking dates and D and fucking V would strike me for the next five fucking months. So I was left out of the reshuffle.

We had found 2 IEDs that day on VP 3, one was surface laid, so easily spotted but the other one was a buried pressure plate, on the outer cordon of the VP 360 drill. It was obvious the Taliban had watched our drills and accounted for it. The poppy harvest was also completed today.

04/05/2012 DAY THIRTY NINE/ THE DAY ARE TOUR REALLY DID START

As predicted the Taliban started their summer offensive today and hit every base in our AO in a coordinated well-orchestrated attacks. I was in bed reading when 2 loud bangs sounded then the repeated sound of gunfire. CP Baray was under attack, I went out to put on my body armour and kit. Mine and Minty's kit had been thrown all over the CP, I couldn't find my helmet or nappy. As a crew we always set our kit out in a line so it was easily accessible. I found my body armour and helmet, but Minty couldn't find his, and Sgt Dean was screaming at him to get into hard cover as he had no kit. Fucking Mr McCullough had panicked when we got hit, and instead of picking up his own kit, he picked up our entire crews kit throwing the parts that were not his in any direction, then went into the ops room. I grabbed my rifle and started firing rounds off from the wall.

The net was going crazy, Jay Walker had come under contact from UGL and small arms. Pan Kalay was getting hit, Molly was on the net, as OP Salat was coming under small arms, CP Langer and OP Tear were getting smashed with small arms. FOB Ouellette was getting blitzed by IDF and movement was cancelled as Sgt Dean wanted to go out in the Mastiffs and take them on. OP Minimise was called and no one had a clue what was going on.

Our other section was with Craig and Mo in FOB
Ouellette and they got smashed. A Chinese rocket had
hit an accommodation block in the FOB, killing Cpl
Andrew Roberts and Pte Ratu Silibaravi, injuring 8
others, all part of the Brimstone call sign. SM Mills was
awarded a MC for his work that day, organising the
casualty's and force protection. 2 of our lads Mo and
Reidy carried the stretchers to the MERTs. *"two
members of Royal Logistics Corps died after the
Taliban fired mortars into Ouellette, the north most
British FOB in the region" (Daily Record).*

We were sporadically contacted all day and I enjoyed
taking different positions in the CP firing rounds off.
During a lull in the day we regrouped and were told the
news from FOB Ouellette, I was gutted. I had spoken to
Craig about it later and he told me that all the injuries on
the casualties had been at chest height, so if they had
been wearing there body armour they would have
survived. A five hundred pound bomb had been dropped

143

on a firing position in Pan Kalay and killed a lot of civilians, a local called to the CP and dropped off body parts at the entrance. He had a mixture of what he said was 6 kids that the bomb had hit.

07/05/2012 DAY FORTY TWO/ COMPLEX AMBUSH

I was on CP guard today, and was running in the tank park. Sporadic gunfire rang out but it was too far away to be aimed at us. A multiple from our checkpoint were confirming an IED at VPs 4-5, with Mr Hoare and Mr McCullough on the wagons. A Bamead team, was confirming what looked to be a hoax IED at the side of the road, and came under contact. This was a classic example of a complex ambush. The insurgents would place an obvious IED for us to get out and inspect. Then a machine gun would fire, machine guns are notoriously hard to aim, so there sound would be used to mask the position of a sniper.

Sgt Dean asked for eight guys from the CP to kit up and go out and draw the fire from the Taliban, there was only 12 of us in the CP so I kitted up and grabbed the ECM Brown, which is the heaviest and got into formation. Crouchy was leading the fire support team, and he was fit as fuck so we smashed out five kms in minutes. The lads were shouting at me as the Mastiffs gunners were not returning fire and providing cover for the Bamma team, Minty and Des were on the guns and every time it kicked off instead of locating the firing position they got their heads down. Freezing in contact is common, so Macca used to just throw Des out of the way and jump on the gun, but the Boss was too polite to do it to Minty.

We came under contact 3 times before we got to our grid. The insurgents were all over the area, this was my first foot patrol and I was sweating. I kept my head though and returned fire giving firing directions and insurgent positions. We got to our agreed upon grid and Sgt Deans feign had worked. The insurgents had decided to take us on and changed the direction of their fire. They were in an ancient village and the village was emptying rapidly. 1RWF NCOs were giving instructions to fire on likely enemy positions, this is an illegal fire order, and I stopped it.

Sgt Dean knelt at the back on the net and we formed a base line across a ridge. The Bamma team came up the back of us and joined on to our baseline. Shots were whizzing past us and everyone had their head down. I stuck my head up and located the firing position, a murder hole in an old clay farm house. I brought the section on the target and an entire infantry sections weapons completely destroyed it. It was literally a wall of lead, followed by UGL. We had an LMG, 2 GPMGs, 2 UGLs and an assortment of rifles. An old station wagon with its windows blacked out pulled up to the position we had wiped out. This was an insurgent ambulance and we allowed them to pick up their dead. The lull then evaporated and we came under contact again, the problem with locating a firing position, is that when you hear a gunshot you know is aimed at you, you get your head down. I seen smoke coming from a wall by a windmill. I brought the section on and give the fire orders. We had been under contact for 4 hours. The section were buzzing and adrenaline was high, the firing position was taken out.

An Apache came to provide air support for our extraction and Sgt Dean brought him on to the position. The pilot said though, that 2 heat signals were there but they were dead, so we bugged out back to the CP. When we got back to base the mini op was deemed a success, we had saved the Bamma team, and took out two insurgent positions. We had been in a lot of contacts but none close to this level. My relationship with a lot of the Welsh improved after that, and I used to wind the rest of the RTR lads up about sitting in the wagon. I spoke to Minty about not providing fire support for the Bamma team, and he said he couldn't get the 50 Cal to work. I told Minty he hadn't returned fire in one contact, and this had to change, he said he had R and R coming up and would come back new and improved.

I spoke to the Boss about it and he said it was noted by everyone in the CP and it was a bad reflection on our section. Pan Kalays gunners, Reidy and Biggsey were flying and the Platoon they were attached too were thrilled with them. Our gunners however hadn't managed to get one round off, the commanders had to step up. The Boss was talking about sending Des back and swapping him for a BCR (battlefield casualty replacement). Des had went out on 2 foot patrols and went man down on both of them 100 yards from the CP gate. Sgt Dean was getting sick of him dodging duties in the CP and wanted him gone. After this the gunners lost their role and were rarely used on the wagon. Commanders commanded from top cover so when it did kick off we could return fire. I was a driver and had fired more rounds from top cover than the 3 gunners put together.

Des kept going man down, and he was booked into the med centre in FOB Ouellette. Nobody bought this, he had no visible symptoms. He spent three days bedded down in the FOB. I got on well with the medic and he told me all his tests came back normal, blood sugar, urine, and that they had no idea what was wrong with him. The medic told me that he spent three days on his PSP and was the first when in the queue at scoff time.

08/05/2012 DAY FORTY THREE/ 5 IEDs

Mr McCullough and I were on the lead Mastiff and he was in the gunner's positions, Minty was on R and R so it was just there was just us two on the headset. Mr Hoare was in the back with members of the ANSF Tiger Team, doing a partnering role. We had found five IEDs on the 611 by 1300 and I was sick of sitting on a cordon, the Boss had fired of over a thousand rounds from top cover and there were shells everywhere. Brimstone were becoming like an attachment to our call sign as they were with us every day. The Tiger Team simply don't have the patience of British Soldiers, and they were going berserk in the back. Every time we stopped they jumped out of the back of the wagon, and started makeshift VCPs were they were taxing the locals of their produce. I was fucking raging over this as I was sitting with two British Army Officers. It looked like we were complicit in their theft.

ANSF

The reason the Taliban came to power was due to corruption from Afghan officials. The local population went to local Taliban religious leaders who prevented

this. The ANSF were a disaster and it was a huge

mistake making us work with them. I had issues with the

Muslim religion due to their attitudes to women,

attitudes to western culture, their intolerance of gay

people and other religions. The level of ANSF

corruption is insane, and every one of them is

homosexual. I have seen Muslim clerics on the TV

saying homosexuality doesn't conform in Islam, this is

nonsense, in a Muslim country it was mandatory. The

ANSF would give the village people a run for their

money. They also kidnapped young boys from local

villages and used them as sex slaves called chi boys (tea

boys). The ANSF who were attached to us waited until

younger troopers/fusiliers were alone in Sangers and

would then go into the Sanger and show them

pornographic pictures. These bases were shared with

ISAF forces, and the government of the day just turns

their back on it.

There is no thief like an Afghan thief and I was in a
scouse regiment. Anything which was not nailed down
the ANSF steals. You had to constantly watch them,
boots, gloves, ipods, socks, anything they could get their
hands on. The insurgents took out a balloon which had
cameras attached to it above FOB Ouellette, we were
getting bugged out to collect it. The ANSF commander
in the FOB said as an act of goodwill he would send his
men out to get it. For some reason the 1RWF OC
agreed and let them. The ANSF retrieved it and then
refused to give it back unless they got $10,000.

The ANSF in Pan Kalay turned their guns on Craig's
wagon, asking for $2000, as 2 of their men were
partnering a VCP where 2 platoon caught a High Value
Target. 2 Platoon were showing them how to conduct a
VCP and they were effectively shadowing the call sign
when they had a hit on the HIDE camera they then
transferred the detainee to torchlight. When the ANSF
commander in Pan Kalay found out about this he liaised

with the local Taliban commander who offered him $2000 for the detainee back. This caused chaos and increased security across the AO. He was effectively telling Craig he either wanted $2000 or the detainee back. Craig was living in the same CP as these people.

There are female soldiers right across the British Army but the main roles that would come into contact with the ANSF would be medics, dog handlers, who go out on foot patrol. The ANSF go crazy when they see a female soldier. If we were driving out of a CP, they would block our paths and stare us out trying to impress the female soldiers. They would follow them around the base, packs of men pointing and yelling. It was so uncomfortable. Female soldiers would avoid going to the gym or fixing their hair, or using any make up or cosmetics due to this.

09/05/2012 DAY FORTY FOUR/ SURFACE LAID IED

Another surface laid IED was found on the 611 today. I was under the belief that the insurgents were watching our drills to develop their attacks. Sometimes the surface laid IEDs were real and this one today was. It was a 20 kilo command wire device which wasn't connected. We must have surprised them. Normally they are hoaxes just placed to sanitise our movements and disrupt the 611. We cordoned it and I just read for a few hours.

10/05/2012 DAY FORTY FIVE/ MAN AWAY DRILLS

We were mobilised for a training exercise today and the AO was buzzing with manpower. We were doing man away rehearsals. Man away drills are to combat somebody going missing from your unit. A live British soldier is much more valuable to the Taliban than a dead one. The risk was that a member of the ANSF would trick a soldier into coming on to their camp and then they would sell them to the Taliban. This rehearsal must have been the exact same as the one they done in the last tour, because on the grid square were we were supposed to be on there was yet another IED. 2 artillery shells were tied together with a wire running to a pressure plate. The Boss was made up that we found another IED, but I knew that we would have to sit here all day until the exercise was over then wait on Brimstone and I wanted to go running.

11/05/2012 DAY FORTY SIX/ WAGON GOES DOWN

Mr McCullough and Molly had went man down with D and V again, Macca was on R and R so we were down a commander. Jay Walker had to come down to our CP to crew a wagon. Jay and I were placed on the rear wagon with Suthers and Sgt Dean on the front wagon. I was made up to be with Jay the only problem was that I had been working on the front wagon for around 2 weeks and it was in superior shape. I had sorted the tyre pressure, filled all the levels and the wagon was spotless. All the paperwork was up to date as where the rations, ammunition, fuel and med kit. I was only ever in the front one as that had the choker but I think Sgt Dean was trying to do me a favour placing me with Jay.

The only problem with this was that the rear wagon was in a shit state. There were fuel problems and it was a mess. I spoke to Sgt Dean and explained that I wasn't comfortable patrolling in it and it had to go to FOB Ouellette as it was a risk not an asset. Sgt Dean just ignored me and we broke down around twenty minutes later. Jay had witnessed me speaking to him and making it clear that I wanted the REME to look at the wagon. I explained to Jay that this was nothing and he always pulled stunts like this. The wagon had been maintained badly and the fuel transfer switch wasn't operational. The REME immediately condemned the wagon and told

Sgt Dean that it wasn't leaving the FOB until it had the all clear.

13/05/2012 DAY FORTY EIGHT/ TIGER TEAM

All week we had been messed around havening to go on patrols with the Tiger Team and it was destroying me. I hated working with them. They would try and sit up the front with me, so instead of watching the road I had to watch these creepy cunts. The Boss would be standing up in the gunners spot and they would be taking photos of his legs. Every time we came into contact they would jump out of the wagon and start firing from the hip in any direction. They would try to light cigarettes in the wagon and I would throw their lighters and crush there cigarettes, they had no manners and I was fucking inflexible with them.

We were patrolling the 611 and came across another surface laid IED. It was a large cylinder with wires attached to a yellow fertiliser bag. I stopped and the Boss started to call it over the net. The Tiger Team in the back, jumped out and started smoking. Normally the Taliban leave an obvious IED then fire at us, everyday this happened. The Tiger Team commander then went up took the cylinder and unattached it from the fertiliser bag as he couldn't be bothered waiting for the Brimstone call sign. He then tried to get in the back of the Mastiff. I told the Boss I was not prepared to drive with unexploded ordnance in the wagon. The Boss was arguing with them through the Terp. The commander was sitting in the back with the cylinder, just brushing him off. Mr McCullough told me to drive back to the CP, but I refused. He then give me a direct order. I told him that he will regret this.

When SM Mills found out that Mr McCullough allowed unexploded ordinance in the back of a Mastiff, he went crazy and tore strips off him on the net. He was to report the FOB Oulette OPS room as soon as the tasking was over. Voice Procedure on the net normally follows a set of guidelines, no names or swearing or raised voices, this went out the fucking window, as this was a very public dressing down.

14/05/2012 DAY FORTY NINE/ SNIPER

I was on guard today and went to do STAG on the Sanger at 0600. This was the best STAG time. 0600 to 0800 is when all the duties in the CP are done, you have to cook breakfast and clean the camp. It's not a massive hassle but if you are on STAG 0400 to 0600 it's a ball ache going straight into it. Fusilier Bradshaw, was giving me a Sanger brief, he was one of the best fusiliers on camp, always early for STAG, and always giving comprehensive briefs. He was explaining arcs to me and recent vehicle movement when the air around the Sanger was suddenly displaced with a whizzing sound. We were coming under sniper fire but had no idea where it was coming from. Bradshaw said he would report it and that it was probably a Dragunov rifle as there were reports of one in the area. He said he would get me breakfast and bring it up and to be careful.

DRAGUNOV SVD

A Dragunov SVD is a 7.62x54mm gas operated rotating bolt semi-automatic sniper rifle. Its effective range with a sight is 1300m.

18/05/2012 DAY FIFTY THREE/ CONTACT CP BARAY

We were exhausted, it was almost routine now to find several IEDs a day then get opened up on. We were just being used for cordons. The 1RWF had cancelled foot patrols in the AO due to the risks from IEDS and sniper fire, so all the infantry could do were VCPs, VPs and CP guard. The RTR Mastiff drivers were getting fragged. Our mission was to keep the 611 open. We were nowhere close to achieving this. The Taliban could close the road in the blink of an eye. You could sit on a cordon at VP 2, wait for five hours and then sit on another cordon on VP 3. A cordon was the use of armour (Mastiffs) to block the road. We would then wait on the Brimstone call sign to come up and detonate a device.

We worked with American bomb disposal experts called war hammer who were rapid. We always hoped they would come out instead of the British bomb disposal team Brimstone. The Taliban were, getting braver, CP Baray was on a hill and had panoramic views of the AO. Out of every CP it was in the most commanding position. We had some contacts but very short, nothing like Pan Kalay or Salat which went on for hours.

This changed at dusk we get hit. The most common times for a base to get hit are at dawn or dusk. This is because attackers can use the cover of darkness to get in place and is the quintessential surprise attack. We had become complacent in the CP and were relaxing. Loud bursts of automatic gunfire ripped through the CP and tracer fire went everywhere. The Taliban were blasting us with PKM and AK47 gunfire. I was under the impression the Taliban didn't use tracer fire, but the red rounds were going everywhere. I was with Suthers and we both got kitted and went for the positions we always took. Suthers was knelt down wearing a helmet, body armour, union jack shorts and flip flops. I had shorts and flip flops on. He was screaming at me to get down as the rounds were bouncing all over the CP. Again the only 2 RTR soldiers on the wall were Suthers and I. Sgt Dean and his NCOs were firing mortars and using section weapons, running the wall giving the lads ammunition, Minty and the Boss were in hard cover.

This was noted after it by the fusiliers, asking me were the rest of our lads were when it kicked off.

PKM

A PKM is a 7.62 General Purpose Machine Gun

designed in the Soviet Union in the 1960s. The PKM

can be used as a light anti-aircraft weapon when it's not

mounted. The effective range of the PKM for

suppressive fire is 800m in the light role, and 1200m in

the sustained fire role. The PKM utilises ammunition in

non-disintegrating belts and ball, tracer and armour

piercing rounds the Taliban have stockpiles of.

AK47

The AK47 is a selective fire, gas operated 7.62mm

assault rifle developed in the Soviet Union by Mikhail

Kalashnikov. The AK47 was one of the first true assault

rifles and due to its durability, low production cost and

ease of use the weapon and its numerous variants

remain the most widely used assault rifle in the world.

After the Soviet retreat from Afghanistan the Soviet

army left quantities of weapons including AKs which have been used by Jihadi fighters ever since.

23/05/2012 DAY FIFTY EIGHT/ RECOILLESS RIFLE OPERATION

A massive OP had been planned for today, it was to locate a recoilless rifle. The 82mm recoilless rifle, is designed to smash through tank armour, it was causing chaos in the AO. Out of the RTR Gwilliam, Molly and I were on it and I couldn't wait. We were getting dropped into a Taliban bed down location at dawn by chinooks, then going on raids of the compounds, it was high risk, but a cracking picture OP. Molly came and spoke to me, he said that Mr McCullough had taken me off the OP, and put Des on it instead. I told Molly this was laughable, he agreed but he said that he couldn't risk putting the lead driver at risk due to the nature of the OP. I went to see Sgt Dean. Sgt Dean and I simply did not speak in the CP. We were professional on the

Mastiff together and he was by far the best commander, but other than that I just blanked him, and several of the other 1RWF NCOs.

He said if Des went man down on this OP or didn't perform he would be camped. I told him Des didn't want to go on it, and that the Boss was just punishing him. Sgt Dean wasn't going on the OP, he had let Mr Hoare on it instead. He told me that I would be missing fuck all, that there would be that much firepower there the Taliban wouldn't strike. He said that I would be put on notice to move in the FOB, in case we had to bug people out as there were over 100 boots on the ground.

The OP was a success in the sense no one got hurt, but no weapons were found and no one was detained. It was a cracking photo OP there were helicopters all over the place, infantry sections everywhere, warrior's, jackals, and all sorts of armour. I wasn't that pissed off as I got breakfast in the FOB, went to the gym, welfare and got a straight six hours sleep. Des had fucked up massively on the OP but it took us a few weeks to find out what.

B-10 RECOILESS RIFLE 82MM

The B-10 Recoilless Rifle is a Soviet 82mm smoothbore recoilless rifle. It was phased out of service in the Soviet Army in the 1960s and replaced by the SPG-9m. The weapon consists of a large barrel with a PBO-2 slight mounted to the left. It is mounted on a small carriage which has two large wheels, which can be removed. It is normally towed by vehicle although it can be towed by its four man crew for short distances. The Taliban will die to protect this piece of equipment and we got hit by it a few times.

25/05/2012 DAY SIXTY/ MAN DOWN CP BARAY

Lance Corporal Owen, Cal got hit with an IED today at VP3, I was gutted as Cal was one of the NCOs I got on with. They were short cutting VP checks as only him and a valon man, were doing the checks, it should be a minimum of five not two. He was always in the gym, along with L/Cpl Balzeratti (Crouchey called him balls are sweaty) and a fusilier called Coy, these are the lads I was spending most of my time with. CP Baray was also hit with PKM fire, and OP Salat got hammered, Molly called through a 500llb which missed its target and Coy and Balz who were on foot patrol had to on their belt buckles.

26/05/2012 DAY SIXTY ONE/ CP LANGER

Captain Stephen Healey, from 1st Battalion, The Royal Welsh, was on patrol in the AO when his vehicle was blown up by a bomb. He was operating with a recce unit out of CP Langer. I was on the phone looking down the 611 and heard a loud explosion there were flames and smoke close to CP Langer. I was on CP Guard so the rest of the lads got mobilised to attend the scene. The Jackal Capt. Healy had been driving in hit a 25kilo pressure plate IED and flipped the wagon. Two of the crew also lost limbs in the incident.

Deaths are always reported, but what is less reported is the loss of limbs which other soldiers face. For every death in theatre there are five lads who have suffered amputations or lost their sight. The top gunner was being seen to by a medic and he was begging the medic to save Capt. Healey. This hit the Welsh in our CP hard. With Cal being hit and now a popular Captain being killed their morale was zero. *"Captain Healey commanded the Combined Force Burma reconnaissance platoon and, whilst conducting a vehicle patrol in the north of the Nahr-e Saraj district of Helmand province, his vehicle struck an improvised explosive device. He was given immediate first aid before being flown to the military hospital at Camp*

Bastion where, sadly, his death was confirmed" (UK Forces in Afghanistan, WordPress). Captain Healey was an ex professional footballer and had played for Swansea.

The SVR which went down to extract the jackal and got hit by a secondary IED, the driver then got out with his valon and he was then hit by another IED. There were also IED finds, in CP Berkshire, OP Salat and OP Tear. The AO was falling apart the road was constantly closed and lads and vehicles were getting hit every few days. The manpower simply wasn't there, and the Yanks were getting pissed off that the road was always closed.

JACKAL

The Jackal is described as a bullet magnet by Squaddies due to it having no protection around the crew. The primary role of the vehicle in the British Army is deep battle space reconnaissance, rapid assault and fire support - roles where mobility, endurance and manoeuvrability are important - and it has also been used for convoy protection. According to the Ministry of Defence, the Jackal "was built to meet the British Army's specific requirements for an agile, well-armed, light patrol vehicle." The vehicle's suspension system provides a more stable firing platform while moving and the 1 metre ground clearance allows it to clear large obstacles. The high levels of off-road mobility enable troops to avoid more conventional routes which may be subject to ambush or enemy reconnaissance.

JUNE

"It is always more difficult to fight against faith than against knowledge."

Adolf Hitler

30/05/2012-20/06/2012 DAY SIXTY FIVE/ PAN
KALAY WAGONS MAN DOWN 504 HR DAY

Suthers left for R and R today, he was a big loss in the
CP. He was the only other driver who was comfortable
on the choker and he would be away for around 21 days.
Pan Kalay had damaged their choker so they could only
do admin runs to FOB Rob which was an American
Base around 200 meters away from their base. Jay
Walker had went back to Bastion with a knee injury,
leaving them a man down, so Craig and Mo got beasted.
Jay wasn't doing well on the tour, he was always
snapping or contracting D and V, or creating another
reason as to why he couldn't go out. With D and V and
his knee he had over three months off and should have
been replaced by a competent BCR (Battle Field
casualty Replacement).

With Pan Kalay not having a choker they refused to
carry out their job role and we inherited their tasking's.

We were already doing considerable hours and now had double the role. They should have asked for the black top tasking's to give us a chance but 2 platoon choose not to do this and sat off in their base for 21 days.

A day consisted of, getting up at 0230 for route domination for two to four hours, then VPs 1to 9, with a turn around 30km away at CP Kamparak Pul, which extended our patrolling ground from 25km to 55km, then we would prove a route to CP Langer and OP Tear. We would then do all the movements across the AO for R and R and any other tasking out of the main FOB. This was on top of cordons, contacts, counter IED and running two bases. Molly and Bob were in OP Salat. Des went man down again and was transferred to the main FOB. He was a spare part on the wagon, he would sit in the commander's chair with no headset on and look out the window. We were staging on a 50 kilo IED, and we were getting sporadic gunfire from Taliban who were circling us on scramblers. We were each taking turns on the gun. Sgt Dean asked Des to take his turn, he was up for five minutes and we came under fire. He said he didn't feel well and that he was seeing spots before his eyes, so Sgt Dean jumped up and started firing.

We had to get the QRF out in warrior's to pick him up, he was brought back to FOB Ouellette and took up his position in the med centre. Sgt Dean said that was it, he was taken off patrols and kept in Camp to do guard duties, just cleaning and stag. We done a simple kit check, when Des was in the med centre and we were down a set of LUCIEs. These are night vision attachments which are connected to helmets'. They are only issued to gunners as there is no necessity for a driver to have them. Everyone in the CP was searching for them. Sgt Dean was stunned that we were down a set and didn't report it. Des had lost them and instead of owning up he pretended either Bob or Mintys set were his, as there were always two sets on the wagons. When either Molly or Macca done a kit check he was able to hold up a set, and he had got away with it for a while. Sgt Dean was carrying out a serialised kit check and when only two were found the numbers were checked and Des was a set down. He wasn't in the CP at the time and Minty was getting the blame, this was unfair as Des was pretending that Mintys set were his.

The Taliban don't operate at night due to having no night vision. We had been getting hit at night for the last few weeks. When we were getting hit, Des would sit in hard cover while the rest of us protected the CP. The loss of this equipment was a huge blow for Mr McCullough, and for our RTR section in general. We got thrashed while Des was sitting off in the med centre. We had to go through every item of kit and search the wagons time and time again. Des had no idea where he lost it but he had been told that if you lose it on an operation, you don't have to pay for it. He said he lost on the recoilless rifle op, but a full itemised kit check took place after that so he wasn't correct, he said he had

put it in with ECM blue when he had been on foot patrol
and when he went man down someone must have stolen
it. Sgt Dean was freaking out and wanted Des on a plane
back to the UK, losing an item this big and then hiding
its loss, was making him look bad. He had just handed
them to the gunners without getting any paper work
signed. Ultimately if you haven't signed for it, you
don't fucking pay for it. Sgt Dean had signed for all the
kit in bulk and it was on his head.

For a reason known only to himself Mr McCullough
wrote a statement saying that the night vision were
issued to him and that he had lost them. This was a
crazy decision, as it had nothing to do with him. They
were issued to Des and he should have took the hit. Mr
McCullough, was charged and fined £1000, and an
entry was put in his tour report. I spoke to him and told
him not to do it, and that it defied logic, but he wouldn't
listen.

On the 02/06/2012 a young Cpl called Cpl Thacker was shot while on duty at observation post Tir. They had come under prolonged contact and Cpl Thacker got hit by a sniper.

"The serviceman, from 1st Battalion, The Royal Welsh, was manning an observation post in the Nahr-e Saraj District of Helmand Province when his patrol came under attack from small arms fire, the ministry of Defence said.

He received immediate medical attention and was evacuated from the scene by helicopter but died of his injuries.

The 27-year-old father-of-one - who was born in Swindon, Wiltshire and had served in Northern Ireland, Iraq and Afghanistan - was described as a "soldier's soldier" and "natural leader" by his comrades."

(Telegraph)

This was a hammer blow to the 1RWF 2 of the most popular and charismatic soldiers in their Regiment had been Killed in Action. The Welsh had undermanned the entire AO and it was getting dangerous. OP Tir had no relevance to the operational role of keeping the 611 open, and was just there so the Taliban could attack it from the green zone. The Welsh were trying to dominate a 50km stretch of road with 2 Mastiffs. Once Cpl Thacker got hit I thought the MOD should have stepped in and pulled their tour. There were around 30 lads sent home with injuries also which where a mixture of IEDs and IDF wounds.

In CP Baray we were really struggling, Gwilliam and I were destroyed and we were effectively running the entire AO on our own, no movement or task could be completed without us. Minty pissed me off big time, he was a trained driver but all he done was sit off in the CP watching DVDs and playing table tennis. He came on the wagon as a gunner and dropped weapon oil all over the back of the Mastiff, he then blamed me for hitting a bump, I was ready to kick him and McCullough apart at this stage, why the fuck did he have an open bottle of weapon oil unsecured in the gunners turret. I spoke to Macca about it and he said, that it was 100% Mintys fault, he said that the fusiliers in the back had complained to Sgt Dean about him and the Boss fucking me over in the wagon, they were also unhappy about both not pulling their weight in camp and this incident just highlighted their weakness.

Sgt Dean asked me about it when I went out on the next patrol, he said that the Boss and Minty were a huge disappointment, I told him it was true that he had unsecured kit in the gunners station and that I would handle it. I didn't like bad mouthing members of my troop to the Welsh and on the wagon Sgt Dean and I had an unwritten rule were we would not discuss each other's staff. We pulled up to do a quick VCP and the wagon was smashed with gunfire. Crouchy had just got out and the Taliban had blitzed him. This was some shooting as the firing point was around a 1.5km away, sparks were hitting my window and bouncing all over the road, the Medic Mason ran to the front of the wagon and the rounds were at his feet. I had never seen such a quick and accurate response by the Taliban before and knew we had been setting patterns. We were that tired we were getting lazy in our drills and for the last four days we had stopped in the same place to run a VCP. Sgt Dean fired around 600 GPMG rounds at the firing point to cover his men, but there was no response from the 50 on the other vehicle as Minty was on it.

I was doing most of my sleeping on the wagon on cordons and it was crazy, I had went from 88 kilos to 60 kilos, almost a third of my body weight. We were starting to get hit a lot in an area down from OP Salat called hoax corner. I was spending around 12 hours a day there. We got contacted from a small village called Satunkay one night and we had to provide cover fire for a Navy Brimstone team. Macca and I were in the wagon and it was hysterical watching their drills. Macca was firing the GPMG and slating the Navy, they were running around in circles, I thought it could be some confusion tactic, as the Taliban stopped firing. The IED wasn't a hoax though it was a 40 kilo command wire device, which was placed close to where we were stopping in our over watch position at night.

Over these 21 days there was a lot of bad feeling being directed towards Craig from the lads based in CP Baray. As the Mastiff commander in Pan Kalay it was his fault they weren't operational and he was seen as a hate figure. Every time he went on the net, the Welsh NCOs would come across after him mimicking his Scottish accent, and trying to make him look stupid. He never recovered from this in the eyes of 1 Platoon.

I spoke to Mr Hoare concerning the hours Gwilliam and I were working and showed him the driver's hour's forms for seven days. Mr McCullough had asked us to doctor them but I refused to do it. I told Mr Hoare that as the 1 Platoon Troop leader he would be held directly responsible for any accidents. He took Gwilliiam and me off the next day placing Minty in the front wagon and Balz in the rear. This proved to be a fucking disaster though as Minty almost rolled the wagon at a turnaround point at VP 7. He had to be recovered and the infantry refused to get in the wagon when he was driving. SM Mills went mental and spoke to Mr McCullough, the Boss told him it was down to driver exhaustion. This was nonsense however as this was the first time Minty had left the CP in days, and I'm sure the Boss told him it was me driving.

Pan Kalay ended up getting a new lead wagon on the 21/06/2012 and could carry out their tasking's again. This was a massive help and halved our workload, and with Suthers coming back soon it would take a weight off. The 1RWF had also sent 8 Soldiers under Training, to our CP who were straight out of Catterick (phase 1 training). This was risky as they had done limited pre-deployment training. One a guy called PO PO from Uganda was a danger to the entire AO, and was camped after two patrols.

22/06/2012 DAY EIGHTY SEVEN/ THE 3 RIFLES A COMPANY

A strike ops team were mobilised from Bastion into our AO today. 3 Rifles A Company were to be housed in CP Baray for two to three weeks. Sgt Deans platoon, and our RTR section were to be relocated to OP Salat and carry out our tasking's from there. OP Salat was built for 8 lads and it would be housing thirty. Mr Hoare and Molly had went on R and R, so Sgt Dean, Mr McCullough and Macca would be commanding. Des had returned from the Med Centre but Sgt Dean did not want to take him with the main body so left him to be a cleaner in CP Baray.

We spent days cleaning and prepping the CP for new arrivals and it was the cleanest and in the best condition it had been in. The 2 Mercian's would have been embarrassed as it was handed to us in a shit state. The 3 Rifles were a sight for sore eyes as they brought up 3 female soldiers who looked and dressed like strippers. 2 medics and an artillery officer, who thought they were in Ibiza. Hot Pants and bikini tops. In fairness though all the lads wore flip flops and shorts as it was that hot. Sgt Dean was complaining that it was a Muslim country and reactions of the ANSF, but I was like fuck it, I have just spent 3 months surrounded by blokes, but in reality he was right.

The 3 Rifles were going to cross into the green zone draw out the enemy and then 900 US Marines were going to go in after and clean up all the Taliban positions. Great in theory. We took them out for a familiarisation patrol just around the CP, so they could get some photos being on the ground and we got contacted. Three Taliban gunmen attacked us with a PKM and 2 ak47s. It went on for around 30 minutes, which feels like a long time, and I had emptied three magazines, 90 rounds. The Rifles were in shock they had only been in the CP for around 2 hours.

WE moved all our kit down to OP Salat in the Mastiffs. It was tiny with a small gym and limited facilities. Sgt Dean had managed to procure a spare welfare phone, so we had two which was a massive help. I had to change my training schedule as there was no running area in the OP. I created a cardio steps program using the rear Sanger steps. It was 40 mins long solid stepping, then 100 press ups and 50 sit ups. I was doing a 40 min steady state in CP Baray followed by 20 mins sprint then 25 sit ups, 25 press ups. This was in 50 degree heat. OP Salat worked out brilliantly and I trained twice

185

a day, I could see why everyone liked it. It was so small it was easy cleaned, there was one STAG point, I had really drew the short straw having to stay in the CP.

A one day on, one day off rota was created by Sgt Dean, which meant it was like a holiday camp, as Gilliam, Balz, Suthers and I shared the driving of the 2 Mastiffs. This was the best time I had on the tour based here.

24/06/2012 DAY EIGHTY NINE/ CARRYING NO ROUNDS IN A WAR ZONE

Mr McCullough was always making mistakes and could be calamitous, his main issue was he never listened to advice. He was always missing grid locations or driving past CPs we were meant to stop at, or a favourite of his was saying contact on the net, if you tried to tell him however he would be short with you. This particular day I had been working on the wagons with the REME all day. Mr McCullough had been in the FOB and was sporadically checking on progress.

I was in no mood as I had been under a wagon all day, with just Gwilliam helping me. The other 10 lads that were with us, just dispersed to use the welfare facilities. When we were leaving I was in the rear mastiff with the Boss and he was positive as we were half way through. I asked him were his grab bag was just as we were leaving the FOB. A grab bag for a tank soldier is an essential item of kit. It is a small bag were you can store rations, sweets, books and drinks. The Boss kept his magazines in them as they were uncomfortable attached to his body armour. He was the only soldier I knew who did this as they had to be on you at all times on the ground.

He had left it in the REME, I told him, just go on the net, tell the lead wagon to pull up on the road, we have to go back into the FOB. Simple. No. I explained to him that he could end up being charged, not to mention the embarrassment it would again bring on the section. According to the Boss it wasn't my concern.

We got back to the OP and within minutes Sgt Dean has put the net on loud speaker and asks Mr McCullough to listen. The SM is asking Sgt Dean to check the Boss for magazines. This was a classic stunt the 1RWF pulled, they know he hasn't got them. When the 1RWF screwed up they just swept it under the carpet, if an RTR lad messed up, they would be jumping up and down on the wagon.

An entire section of lads had to re-kit, and bug out to the FOB to collect his mags. I was embarrassed for him, as this was a huge blunder, and he hadn't made a public one in a while. We went back to the FOB in silence. He had to go to the Ops room and pick his bag up. I think they told him that mistakes happen and to be more careful.

25/06/2012 DAY NINTY/ WHERES YOUR WEAPON

I was on the lead wagon with Mr Hoare as commander and we got a message through on the net to collect a rifle which had been left in Pan Kalay. The owner of the rifle was in FOB Oulette, 25kms away. It was Trooper Tucker from our other section. There is nothing worse for a soldier than to lose his weapon, magazines is serious but not that serious. Tucker had made a few mistakes, losing his day sack full of mags and bedding, reversing a Mastiff over a sections kit, from messing about. He was also close to Brown and I believed that both shouldn't have been taken.

Mr McCullough was furious, we hadn't picked up the rifle yet and the infantry were already giving us a hard time, concerning our abilities as soldiers. He was going to formally charge Tucker and try to take away a percentage of his tour bonus. I spoke to him and told him that Tucker in theory could defend the charge, and use his loss of magazines as a defence. He about turned and said he would speak to him. For the rest of our time with the 1RWF this was brought up whenever we argued and I hated Tucker for it. No matter how hard you worked, you were always judged by the other people in your cap badge. Also when Tucker went on R and R he tried to take a bayonet onto the plane, the kid was just lazy.

SA 80 A2 L85

The SA80 A2 L85 is a 5.56mm gas-operated assault rifle manufactured by Heckler & Koch. It is a member of the SA80 family of assault weapons and serves the British Armed Forces as Individual Weapon (IW) and Light Support Weapon (LSW).

The SA80 series of rifles entered service with the British Army in 1985. The SA80 family underwent a major mid-life update in 2002, during which the SA80 A1 rifles were upgraded to the SA80 A2 standard.

CP BARAY REAR MASTIFF

LEAD MASTIFF WITH CHOKER INTACT CP
BARAY

CP BARAY GYM

OP SALAT 611 HELMAND

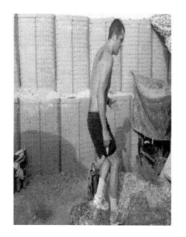 

OP SALAT   CP BARAY

TRYING NOT TO GET STUCK

JAY WALKER GETTING RECOVERED IN
BARKSHIRE

CHURCH FOB OULETTE (by the end it was covered
in gold plaques)

SGT DEAN AND CROUCHEY CONTACT CP
BARAY

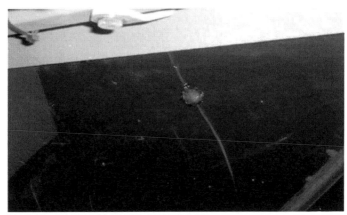

TALIBAN TRYING TO SHOT ME

MY BEDSPACE ON THE RIGHT/ MASON WAS ON
THE LEFT GYM WORKOUT OP SALAT

ANOTHER MISSING CHOKER

CONTACT OP SALAT

BRIMSTONE TEAM 611

SUTHERS/ GWILLAM/ MINTY/ MOLLY/
MACCA/ SHEILDSEY/ ME /BOB

611BLACKTOP

FOB OULETT TOP /REIDEY/CRAIG/ ME/MR
MCCULLOUGH(still in osprey)/ SANO/DOYLEY

BOTTOM/ BIGGSEY/ DES/ MOLLY/ JAY

VP CHECKS EVERYDAY

AIR SUPPORT CONTACT 611

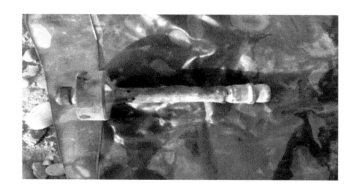

107 MORTOR CP BARAY

FOB OUELETTE BALOON   L/CPL MASON
RAMC

CLOSING THE 611 KAMPARAK PUL

KAMPARAK PUL, SGT DEAN, MACCA AND I
DESTROYED THIS WITH GPMG AND 50CAL
FIRE, THERE WERE A TOTAL OF THREE
SHOOTERS IN THE SANGER

IED 35TH BIRTHDAY I WAS IN THE DRIVERS
SEAT JUST ABOVE THE BLAST (gwilliam)

29/06/2012 DAY NINTY SIX/ IED BERKSHIRE

I was in the gym in OP Salat and heard a distant bang, then another one in quick succession, I was hoping for an own goal, "IED man down, man down", "IED, IED, IED", this was bad, I got my kit on body armour, rifle, helmet, and went out to the wagon. The lads were panicking as they had been through an awful time with Capt Healy and Cpl Thacker, the 1RWF were white. Sgt Dean was waiting for the go ahead and we were on immediate notice to move. This meant we were sitting in the vehicles in our crew positions, engine running.

News started to filter through that a young welsh fusilier on his first patrol had been hit, then someone went to help him and he got hit. It was chaos, CP Berkshire was across desert and was only accessed by tracked vehicles. We had went there before but there was always a risk. The MERT response team had picked the casualties up and Brimstone were mobilised to clear the area, we were not on QRF, and so we stood down.

We were drip fed news all day, there was an OP Beak Soldier with the patrol whose dog had not picked up either of the 2 IEDs, it worked out it was a Trooper from 1RTR A SQN. This was another embarrassment, as the 1RWF just hated us for this. The Trooper involved in this was on his first patrol as well and refused to go on the ground again so the AO was an OP Beak down, meaning all of us were losing an IED dog, putting more people at risk.

JULY

"History shows that there are no invincible armies."

Joseph Stalin

01/07/2012 DAY NINETY EIGHT/ KAMPARACK PUL

We were out doing counter IED patrols on the 611, we had reveilled at 0400 and it was approaching 1100, Sgt Dean, Suthers, Mason the medic, Nurse and a fusilier called Rush, were in the lead choker wagon. Macca and I plus 3 fusiliers, Groves, Davis, and Reynolds who were on their first patrol were on my wagon. We were having a bit of a laugh playing eye spy and asking them about Phase 1 training. We were telling them war stories of sitting on the 611 for 40 hours doing nothing.

The net started going crazy, it was just screaming static and gun shots, Sgt Dean started to take off and we followed on. We could not hear what was going on, but someone had been attacked at Kamparak Pul, it was around 30 kms away. I followed Suthers, he was smashing it down the 611. There are normally places where we would slow down due to the ground being broken up and rattling the Mastiff and crews. This wasn't happening, he was driving with the choker in speeds excess of 65kms per hour.

As we got closer the reception on the net improved. A PMAG (police military assistance group) had come under attack at a faraway check point Kamparack Pul which was manned by ANCOP. A green on blue attack. We had worked with them a lot and they had stayed with us in CP Baray. They were Welsh Guards and a mixture of other regiments. The net was improving and from the bits we could pick up there had been a green on blue attack that was ongoing in the CP. As we approached Macca was briefing the lads in the back, the 3 brand new fusiliers who were on their first patrol that we were driving into a close quarter combat situation, and there were casualties. When we approached there was a large boom, an RPG (Rocket Propelled Grenade) was fired as an airburst (distance to explode dial), at our vehicle. The easiest way to describe what was happening was like a scene from black hawk down. On approach the noise was getting louder and louder the sound of machine gun fire was growing. There was no direction from the net, Sgt Dean and Macca are not cowboys and were asking for aiming points. There were 2 Huskies (4 wheel Mastiffs), and a jackal. Rounds were flying everywhere. I got eyes on the firing point, it was coming from the main Sanger, I give the instruction straight away, Macca asked me if I was sure, I said yes and he let rip at the Sanger, 100s of rounds form a 50 cal. Sgt Dean followed suit with his GPMG.

The lads jumped out the back of our wagon and met up with the lads out the back of Sgt Deans. The PMAG were all over the place, the driver of one of the Huskies was trying to reverse through the wall of the CP. There were 3 firers in the Sanger with automatic weapons, and a section of men to the east providing fire for them.

The lads off the wagons were giving CPR to the injured and the dead. There was sprays of blood all over the white washed walls of the CP, and the plaster was flying every time the ANCOP fired at our lads. The gunfight was continuing and slowly but surely the Sanger started to get destroyed. An Apache appeared and annihilated the section of ANCOP to the east with waves of fire. Instructions were coming over the net but we could hear nothing and Macca told me to jump on the gun to cover the lads while he sorted comms. I was used to jumping up with my rifle to provide cover fire from the hatches, on a reload, not firing the main weapon. I was straight up blitzing the Sanger, the ANCOP were losing heart now that an Apache was mobilise. Groves opened the back door and asked for a stretcher, Macca jumped back on the gun, and I got the stretcher.

An injured soldier was put in the back of Sgt Deans Mastiff, then a body was put in the back, then another 2 bodies were lifted in stretchers, I was expecting one to get in the back of mine, but orders blared over the net to provide cover fire for a casualty run up the 611. Macca and I were left to fight the ANCOP. A chinook pulled in and landed on the 611 around 200 meters away from our position. I seen the lads doing the stretcher runs using Suthers Mastiff as a shield and we provided the fire power to get the ANCOPS heads down. Then a warrior from Lashaek Gar appeared, and started firing salvos of 30mm radon cannon at the Sanger. We had firmly took the advantage and now the ANCOP were starting to back down.

We went into the CP and there were 4 ANCOP 1 was lying down covered in blood. The PMAG were discussing the ANCOPs role in CP Kamparak Pul and I believe the tone of the conversation was how they could improve, as they were notorious for kidnapping boys. The ANCOP took offence and started to pray. As the PMAG were leaving and their backs were turned they opened up on them shooting the last four in the section, automatically killing three and injuring one. This was beyond cowardly as the ANSF would never take on an

ISAF soldier fairly. Guardsmen Craig Roderick and
Apete Tuisovurua, of the 1st Battalion Welsh Guards,
and Warrant Officer Class Two Perran Thomas, of the
Royal Corps of Signals were shot dead that day.

More and more ISAF started to arrive and take over the
carnage. It was night time and we went back to FOB
Ouellette to regroup. The SM spoke to us and told us the
Welsh Guards wished to thank us, for trying to save
their lads, but the three who died were dead before they
hit the ground. The SM told us that we had to go back
and block the 611 as it was chaos there. It was 0100 and
we had been up from 0330 from the night before. Sgt
Dean bought our wagon, five packets of cigarettes, and
we got crates of ice water. We agreed that we would
block the road at the bridge next to the CP to the south
and Sgt Dean would be a km away to the North. I spoke
to Suthers he was in a bit of shock, the back of his
wagon was covered in blood and other bits. I helped
him clean up and got back in.

"Three British soldiers have been killed

in Afghanistan by a gunman wearing a police uniform

who opened fire on them as they prepared to leave a

checkpoint.

In what appears to have been the latest "green-on-blue"

incident, the gunman shot the three troops at checkpoint

Kamparack Pul in Nahr-e-Saraj, Helmand province,

during what should have been a routine visit on Sunday

afternoon. All three were treated at the scene, but died

from their injuries, the Ministry of Defence said.

The soldiers – two of whom were serving with the 1st

Battalion Welsh Guards and one with the Royal Corps

of Signals – had been working in an Afghan police

advisory team and had been conducting a "shura", or

consultation, with their colleagues. Next of kin have

been informed.

In a statement, the MoD said the gunman struck as the

three soldiers were preparing to leave. The suspect, who

was also injured, is in custody. It is believed he is a member of the Afghan National Civil Order Police (Ancop), a special unit set up in 2006 and regarded as much more professional and highly-trained force compared to locally recruited officers." (The Guardian)

I knew it was a bad idea for us to take up the southern position, as Macca was only a lance jack and we were going to be busy. We took up our post, and we thought we would block the road and provide a STAG. That changed almost immediately, the 5 of us had to get out and arrest 14 ANCOP. Then we had to provide three lads for a guard on the detainees. As a driver you are not supposed to leave the wagon, I had no choice as there was no organisation, at the CP. Macca was effectively running the biggest crime scene in Herrick 16 and the Welsh Guards RSM, and the entire RMPs were going through him.

I blocked the road with no commander and jumped out to help. Inside the CP blood was everywhere, and shells were all over the place, there were seven obvious firing points, so the story that the lone firer was receiving treatment in FOB Ouellette for his wounds was non-sense. We went back and took up our post on the wagon. There was only Macca and I left to STAG on the gun, we had now been up for over 24 hours. I was falling asleep across the 50 Cal standing up and dawn was breaking. We were doing 2 hours on two hours off. The 3 lads we had provided for detainee guard had escorted them back to Bastion. So we were on our own. Sgt Dean had piggy backed on the back of a convoy up to FOB Ouellette and got breakfast and fuel and was now back to the north. It was 0800 and every time I woke up there was somebody different sleeping on the Mastiff floor. It ranged from RSMs, RMPs, Intelligence Officers, and random light dragoons.

Somebody was shaking my foot to wake me up and it was a Terp I knew from the start of tour. I hadn't seen him in months, he was trying to tell me that I was wanted by an officer. I asked the Officer what he wanted and he asked me to move the wagon. I moved to the side of the road and our STAG continued. We swapped all day long and the stag eventually ended around 0600 on the next day. We had went out on tasking's on Sunday at 0400 and were returning back to base at 0600 on the Tuesday. When we were returning to OP Salat we were passing the OP Tir and CP Langer turn in's, and the Ops room in FOB Ouellette asked us to prove the route with the choker. That was the Welsh all over they could not give a fuck about their lads, a shit OC and 2IC, had destroyed the ranks of 1RWF.

When we had got back to the OP, most of the lads had moved back to CP Baray as the Rifles OP had ended. Nice of them to leave all the weight for us to take. Sgt Dean said we had five admin hours before we moved and I got my head down in the middle of the Afghan sun, I was shattered. Some of the lads didn't sleep though, they sat up trying to make some sense of it.

Macca woke me up and told me to get my kit on the wagon, I got sorted. I was sorry to be leaving Salat, as it was easy street. When I got back to CP Baray Minty and the Boss were sitting off in shorts and flip flops. Des was there, but as soon as we got in Sgt Dean spoke to him and was transferring him to OP Dara, just an easy tasking for two weeks before his R and R. This was to protect the morale of the CP.

We had to take him down to FOB Ouellette, and then transfer him a few hundred meters to the OP which was just a post to overlook the green zone. We then returned to the CP. The Rifles had destroyed the CP, the toilets and the showers were a mess and they had wrecked the kitchen. The Boss had let the Rifles walk out of there without tidying up. Sgt Dean was going crazy and tried to get in touch with the 3 Rifles SM to send his lads back. We found the Dixie's, the pots and pans used for cooking and they hadn't cleaned them. This in military terms is viewed the same as cowardice, to trash a camp and let another unit it clean it up is just not done, and this is the first time I had ever heard of it. Sgt Dean was blaming Mr McCullough and so were the lads who were doing the cleaning, but by this stage what else did you expect. I cleaned up for a few hours and went to bed, the tour was getting to me.

FOOT NOTE

One of the reasons for writing this book, was that neither Sgt Dean nor L/Cpl McNeill received any recognition for their actions that day. Sgt Dean was responsible for the transportation of three KIA (killed in action) a walking wounded, onto an air transport under fire, not to mention winning a fire fight against superior numbers. Macca took control of the biggest incident in

Herrick 16, and effectively was responsible for the
detention of fourteen ANCOP who were the guilty
parties. Mr McCullough put no mention of this day in
my tour report. A 1RTR soldier had not been involved in
anything of this scale for years. There is a lot of petty
jealousy in the Army, and people don't like others out
shining them, especially Troopers.

RPG 7

The RPG 7 is a widely produced, portable shoulder
launched anti-tank rocket propelled grenade weapon.
Originally the RPG 7. The ruggedness, simplicity low
cost and effectiveness of the RPG 7 have made it the
most widely used anti-tank weapon in the world. The
most commonly seen variations are the RPG 7D and the
lighter Chinese type 69 RPG.

L/CPL MASON RAMC

Crochey might have been the best soldier in camp but L/Cpl Mason was easily the bravest. The guy was an uber camp Medic and he had a hell of a tour, he was always the first to get involved in every situation. He tried to resuscitate two soldiers at Kamparak, and carried a stretcher under fire. I think he was over looked as well due to petty jealousy from people who were not involved. He used to walk our vehicles into CPs and FOBs singing it's raining men.

TRIM TRAUMA RISK MANAGEMENT

Soldiers run the risk of operational stress through the pressure of deployment and their possible exposure to extremely traumatic situations and events. It is Army policy that mental health issues be properly recognised and treated, and that all efforts are made to reduce the stigma associated with them.

In addition to both pre- and post-deployment briefings, the Army has a system in place called Trauma Risk Management (TRiM.) It is not a medical process, or therapy - it is designed to identify service personnel at risk after traumatic incidents.

Soldiers are often reluctant to talk to strangers when they are in difficulty, and often it is their mates whom they turn to for help. For this reason, TRiM is delivered by trained people already in the affected soldier's unit.

TRiM-trained personnel undergo specific training in the management of people after traumatic incidents. Those who are identified as being at risk after an event are invited to take part in an informal interview which establishes how they are coping.

The process is repeated after a month and a comparison of the outcomes is made, allowing early identification of those who may be having problems so that help can be given early. MOD WEBSITE

SM Mills came to the CP soon after this event and discussed it with us (TRiM brief), I was about to go running, but out of respect for the SM I attended the brief. A TRiM brief starts with what you were doing beforehand, and then develops step by step through the incident until you are back safely. SM Mills included everyone, and each person followed on from one another. The SM makes an informed decision after that whether you are operationally mentally fit for deployment. 2 of the young fusiliers failed the brief and were eventually reassigned.

04/07/2012 DAY ONE HUNDRED AND ONE/ RSM

We pulled into FOB Ouellette and the 1RTR RSM walked past us, we had no idea he was there, so the Boss went to get him. Mr McCullough had arranged for us to sit in the cookhouse and have a discussion with him, he also told us not to be negative and try and put a good light on things. This is what I hated about 11 Troop any time we were meeting someone in rank, we were always briefed to put a gloss on issues. I just thought what's the fucking point of him coming up here if we are just going to blag him. Suthers said *"it's good to see a black beret"*, whether he said it as a joke or not it silenced everyone, and the RSM didn't know where to look. This is the first time I had met the RSM and he was sound. Mr Dunlop was 1RTR through and through and got on to the fact that we must have been briefed to be positive. He was everything you imagine a RSM to be. RIGID.

Mr McCullough was sitting there so I couldn't let rip, but I did question as to why D SQN were living the life of it in Bastion and we were arguing over ration boxes. He admitted it was difficult but it was the only way to get 2 SQNs out here. I also asked him why other troops in G SQN were having the life of it, in FOBS and well equipped bases and we were in shit, and that we felt totally disconnected from any rank structure in 1RTR. We had seen on social media, our other Troops swimming and using air conditioned gyms. At the start it was okay but half way through, it was starting to bite. The RSM knew the 1RWF were very difficult to deal with and knew how bad we were getting it from contact reports and air support in the AO. It was clear to me that the Boss was painting a rosy picture of CF Burma back to our RHQ and I was fucking sick of it.

I questioned him about the authority to go on foot patrol, as we were not trained. My main issue was that they refused to dual role so why should we? The 1RWF CO had begged our CO for assistance and had asked him at a party, when he was probably pissed and that's where it came from. When I told him that only three of us had done it, he said that it was nonsense. Mr McCullough was raging that I had deviated from script, he clearly had been bigging his role and authority up, I hated stuff like this. The Boss was wrong the RSM did want to hear gripes and wanted honesty, what we give him was bullshit and he knew it.

RSM

Regimental sergeant major (RSM) is an appointment held by warrant officers class 1 (WO1) in the British Army, the British Royal Marines and in the armies of many Commonwealth and former Commonwealth nations, including Ireland, Australia and New Zealand; and by chief warrant officers (CWO) in the Canadian Forces. Only one WO1/CWO holds the appointment of RSM in a regiment or battalion, making him the senior warrant officer; in a unit with more than one WO1, the RSM is considered to be "first amongst equals". The RSM is primarily responsible for maintaining standards and discipline and acts as a parental figure to his or her subordinates.

07/07/2012 DAY ONE HUNDERED AND FOUR/
1RWF LOSE PATIENCE

I was out from 0400 on the wagons and arrived back in
CP Baray around 1200. Molly and Mr McCullough
were commanding and Macca and Des were in OP
Salat. I was shattered and wanted a few hours' sleep. As
soon as I got out I knew something was wrong. The
Welsh were gathering around the back of the wagons
and Sgt Dean asked to speak to Molly.

An underslung torch attachment for a SA80 rifle was
found in a box which was being thrown out. The items
serial number was checked and it was issued to Des who
was 15km away in OP Salat. Your torch is supposed to
be a permanent attachment and Sgt Dean wanted to
know why it was not on his rifle. When somebody
makes a mistake or does something wrong in the Army
of a low rank everyone gets punished.

We were told to meet at the front of the Mastiff in 10 mins to discuss Troop discipline. Mr McCullough and Molly didn't know what to say. I pointed out that it was nothing to do with us and regardless of rank, each individual should be responsible for their own kit. The 1RTR NCOs were already not allowed to do kit checks, due to the loss of the night sight. This was another massive embarrassment, but at least the item wasn't lost and they had found it.

We went on patrol later that day and got back into the CP around 2100, Sgt Dean was waiting again and asked to speak to Molly. Molly then asked to us to meet him in ten minutes at the wagon with all our body armour. We all met with kit but Minty couldn't find his. A set of Osprey (body armour) had been found ripped to shreds at the exit to the CP. I had ran over it in my Mastiff, as there were choker marks on the inside.

There was a strict instruction that no item of kit was to left on the Tank Park. This was due to the risk of it being destroyed by AFVs (armoured fighting vehicles), Tucker had wrecked around six sets in Pan Kalay. Body armour was meant to be secured on your person or by your bed space. The fucking mystery was Minty hadn't been on patrol for days, so it didn't make any sense. He tried to blame me, but I just laughed and said good luck with that. Everyone wanted to know how his body armour ended up on the Tank Park as he wasn't out. He admitted what happened, he thought he was on patrols at 0400, so he set his kit behind the wagon, before he went to bed. As he wasn't on patrols the runner didn't wake him, and he had forgot about it. He was 20 hours in the CP without having a clue where his body armour was.

Sgt Dean was going to report Minty and Des to the SM for what took place. The Welsh in the CP were hating us at the minute because they were always getting briefed.

Minty couldn't leave the CP now due to the integrity of his body armour. He needed new plates. I thought Sgt Dean was being over dramatic but he was just losing patience with the mistakes our section were making this late in. Mr McCullough was devastated he knew the SM and OC would be asking him why his lads were ignoring SOPs (standard operating procedures) in the AO. Not having a rifle attachment and leaving your body armour out were going to embarrass the Troop.

10/07/2012 DAY ONE HUNDERD AND SEVEN/ RC IED STRIKE ANCOP

An ANCOP patrol got hit on the 611 as we were driving down the road. The Taliban detonated an RC IED and scored a direct hit on an ANCOP Humvee. It was around 50 meters from VP 3 which we had completed earlier that day. The ECM on the wagon had worked and they waited until the ANCOP came past.

The Humvee was destroyed and on its side. The ANCOP were running around in circles. There was blood everywhere. Two were badly injured and needed air lifted. As soon as we got out of the wagon, rounds started flying everywhere. We couldn't PID (positively identify), the firing point as there were so many rounds. The ANCOP were becoming animated and starting to blame us for their predicament. Mr Hoare was asking for stretchers but there weren't any on the wagons as we had used the four we were issued. I had asked Mr McCullough and a 1RWF NCO for more but they always give me the run-around. Even if I had them, I didn't want to give them to the ANCOP. The ANCOP started to fight amongst themselves and they were raising weapons threatening our lads on the ground. Mr Hoare put the injured in the back of the Mastiffs, I was raging as I would have to clean up after them.

We went down to FOB Ouellette and called in a MERT. The injured ANCOP were transferred to Bastion for treatment. Mr Hoare tried to have a go concerning the stretchers, but I told him to look at his own NCOs who we had to go through for medical equipment and rations. They were that difficult to deal with and so used to fucking you off, I would ask once and not go near them again. Mr Hoare allowed these difficulties to carry on as Sgt Dean seemed to enjoy them. There was blood all over the back of the wagon, it would be me cleaning that, no one else.

12/07/2012 DAY ONE HUNDRED AND NINE/ 5 IEDS

I was now on guard and I was ready for it. We got that thrashed on Patrols, it was nice to get a break. I had done a 0200-0400 stag so I had just stayed up and had went running, cleaned my clothes, cooked breakfast and cleaned the camp. Mr Hoare was on guard as well and he had STAGGED on the camera system and net. He called me in and showed me a mini tour video he had made that night. A tour video is a collection of photos and video footage of big events that happen on tour, edited together then, a soundtrack goes over it. I have seen some brilliant and professional ones. The only thing was when it all really did go off, the last thing you thought about was getting your camera out and recording, so you missed all the best ones.

He had a Red Hot Chilli Pepper track over his and to make it in a CP was an achievement. We scanned the ground in front of the Check Point and just out of view of the Sanger in dead ground next to the road was a yellow plastic container with wires attached to it, an IED. Mr Hoare sent it through on the net. Zero wanted it investigated so I had to wake the patrols lads. The commanders going out were Mr McCullough and Macca. Nobody is happy when you wake them and tell them they are going out to set up a cordon on an IED. As they were getting ready to go out we rescanned the front of the CP, directly facing the CP were the ANCOP had a STAG position was a DFC (Directional Fragmentation Charge), across the road and around 10 meters up was another yellow carton IED.

As the lads were mounting the wagons we seen another yellow carton IED down from the Check Point. This day was going to be a disaster. I was so glad I was on Guard, it took Brimstone an average of four to ten hours to deal with one IED and now there was four. The lads were out without breakfast just as dawn was breaking around 0530, Brimstone wouldn't come until after scoff in the FOB, at least another two hours. While Mr Hoare was making his tour video, four IEDS were planted at the front of the CP.

Not only did the Mastiffs from CP Baray have to go on the cordon but also the Mastiffs from Pan Kalay. The road being blocked like this just as the goods were going to market in Sangan, was going to be a disaster.

Around an hour into the cordon beginning a huge convoy of ANSF were coming from the south to carry on through Sangan. The insurgents obviously knew this and had set up the whole drama. Once the ANSF had come to a standstill the insurgents started to fire. Rounds were going in every direction and the ANSF didn't even try to find the point of fire. The contact was intermittent though as the insurgents were bugging out on vehicles and taking up different positions.

Brimstone had eventually arrived after around four hours. The ANSF have no patience and for some unknown reason Mr McCullough went out and try to reason with them. He was speaking to the Ops room in FOB Ouellette on the net and we sat around the Ops room in CP Baray listening. Zero was telling Mr McCullough under no circumstances were the ANSF allowed to break the cordon and travel up the road. The reason given if an IED detonated and injures one of them they would have to use our MERTs to take them to Bastion. This was a fair point. The ANSF were having none of this and were browbeating Mr McCullough. Zero told the Boss to deal with it and that other people had jobs to do and to stop tying up the net. I almost fell off my chair when I heard this. All Mr McCullough had to say was you're not going up and close the Mastiff, if they go up they have done so without permission. He never learns though and gets back on to Zero in around five minutes, the Ops room OC immediately loses patience and tells the Boss that after the task he had to report to the FOB.

All day long there was firing and I could tell the ANSF were losing interest as only a few of them were returning fire. Our lads only fired if they could PID (positively identify) the target. Brimstone had worked quite quickly and had dealt with three IEDs by around 1800 and then boom an IED goes off, but it wasn't one of the four, it was a hidden one at the entrance to our CP. It created a bit of confusion as nobody had set it off and it didn't hit anyone. It panicked the Brimstone team as they had Bamma that area and didn't pick it up. At around 2200 they had completed their drills and reopened the road, instead of our multiple driving back in, they had to go to the FOB so the Boss could get gripped.

14/07/2012 DAY ONE HUNDRED AND ELEVEN/ OC VISIT

We were in Fob Ouellette when the OC arrived but we were just bugging out to do an admin run so we arranged for the other multiple to collect him. The Pan Kalay Mastiffs went down to collect the G SQN OC from FOB Ouellette Major Ford. He was trying to get out to see us for weeks but was struggling due to transport. Mr McCullough had went on R and R so Molly was the highest 1RTR rank in the CP. The Boss couldn't brief the lads to play incidents down and Molly wanted us to be honest as he was starting to argue each day with them. Major Ford had arrived around 1300 and every 1RTR lad in the CP arranged to wear our regimental t-shirts, which are black, and are the colours of 1 and 2 RTR.

The Welsh were raging about this, and it was designed to show the division in the CP. Major Ford explained that the other troops were busy, but experiencing nothing like we were. The other troops were not doing STAG, or involved in as much SAF (small arms fire), or going on foot patrol, or living in CPs, or Ops, or any IED strikes. This got every ones back up and I could see that the OC wasn't finding it comfortable. We were effectively living in shit, being treated like shit, no protection from our troop leader, and he was telling us that the other troops were having a hard time. Nobody wanted to hear this, he hadn't a clue what was going on in CF Burma. Because the Boss was struggling he wasn't passing anything back to our RHQ, petty jealousy always came into it.

I explained that the 1RWF were rotating their patrols through the wagons, while keeping the drivers on every patrol. This was when they had three drivers in the CP who they refused to use. I explained Minty was a trained driver, and that he wasn't used. Also that dealing with the 1RWF rank structure in the CP was like pulling teeth. Sgt Dean and the NCOs who hung around him were always fucking us over with shit jobs, and McCullough walked away from every argument that I was having over the 1RWF behaviour. Major Ford said we had drew the short straw. The 1RWF had come out dangerously undermanned and ill prepared. They had nowhere near the manpower or the vehicles to run the AO. They had back loaded their Tour with almost 50 guys just out of training and they had put everyone in the AO at risk.

He knew it was bollacks, he was careful with his words and terms but he knew. I enjoyed talking to the OC as he wasn't there to be lied to, he had a genuine interest in

237

the welfare of the lads. Molly and I took him out on a black top patrol. On cameras at night. The OC was buzzing and sat up front with us having a laugh, he give us the generic don't be complacent speech and "for fucksake come home in one bit". We dropper the OC back to the FOB to get his transport back to Bastion. It was the first constructive conversation I had had, since being on the ground. I knew it wouldn't affect change but at least the people who should know, now knew what was going on.

19/07/2012 DAY ONE HUNDRED AND FIFTEEN/ GIVE THE 1RWF A DRESSING DOWN

Sgt Dean and Mr McCullough had went on R and R. Mr Hoare and Molly were running the CP. With those two gone and the CP being a section up from the new arrivals life on the 611 was improving. I had implemented a rota which put the RTR drivers 2 on, 1 off with no STAGs and it was really working out. A visible tension had lifted and the monotony of the 611 was breaking. I was really into my fitness as I was training for a race in August on my R and R. I was 100 % focused and was running for two hours a day.

Suthers, Gwilliam and I were in my bed space talking and a 1RWF fusilier came in and asked two of the drivers to get ready we were mounting up. Gwilliam and I got ready and wondered what was going on as it was just after lunch and are next patrol was at 1600. When we got out there, there were ten Welsh soldiers all kitted up and standing at the backs of the wagon. They were saying we had been bugged out for an IED cordon and Gwilliam and I were holding it up. This was a Sgt Dean classic, get his lads ready then send someone for us to try and make us look unprepared. It was identical to the difficulties for getting rations or any kit through Welsh NCOs. We even had problems getting ammunition for the weapons, this was a gunners job, but are gunners were shocking so drivers did it. You would have to go through a complex requesting system with the Welsh when the ammo store was ten feet away.

Mr Hoare was there and I asked him what he was playing at and that if we were getting bugged out did he not think to inform the drivers as they couldn't go without us. He was ashen faced, I told him the 1RWF stunts were beneath the 1RTR and we choose not to stitch his lads up when they made mistakes, NDs, no batteries for ECM, graffiti in sangers, late for STAG, only we were above their stunts and this was fucking pathetic. He said it was a genuine mistake but this was the tip of the fucking iceberg and because McCullough was shit they could get away with murder. I hadn't argued with Mr Hoare before one of the few people in the CP I hadn't clashed with, but I was in no mood for silly games.

20/07/2012 DAY ONE HUNDERED AND SIXTEEN/
RAMADAN

The Muslim festival of Ramadan started today and the
ANCOP and the interpreters in our CP are beginning to
fast and increase their prayers. Ramadan consists of
approximately a month of fasting which then culminates
in the festival of Ede. Muslims do not eat from dawn
until dusk. The ANSF in our AO are going crazy and
firing rounds and throwing grenades. We have no idea if
we are getting contacted or not. Security is increased in
the CP due to this and we have been put on alert. An
Interpreter told us that Jihadi fighters are rewarded more
in paradise if they die in Ramadan.

We are expecting increased attacks and have been
warned not to trust the Muslims who have been sharing
the CP with us. The Terps had mobile phones and every

time the CP got hit they would be in hard cover minutes before the attack. I simply didn't trust them.

There had been an incident in the CP where the 1RWF Fusiliers had been stealing from the Terps shop. He had a small stand were he sold cigarettes and cold drinks. He didn't have the ability to lock the shop so they just simply took whatever they wanted. He was down around $30 and told everyone that if he didn't get the money that the Taliban would overrun the CP as stealing from him was dangerous. I can't believe he was allowed to stay in the CP but the rank just ignored it. This was the guy who said he preferred boys to women as his didn't like women's bits. Why ISAF employees these people I have never understood.

26/07/2012 DAY ONE HUNDRED AND TWENTY FIVE/ CONTACT OP ARCHER

We had been getting fragged all week as Sgt Dean was back. He changed the whole system as he was fuming that things were going so well. Molly was starting to see what a little Hitler he really was. As OP Salat wasn't operational anymore Molly was dealing with the 1RWF rank structure in CP Baray every day and started to understand just how badly the 1RWF were treating us. He was four fucking months too late. Every idea which an RTR soldier had was immediately shot down, no matter how it improved the lives of people in the CP.

As Mr McCullough was on R and R, Molly had to deal with them as I simply blanked them. Every time he attempted to implement anything on the wagon it was changed at the last minute and Sgt Dean pulled rank, the guy was unbelievable. We would all be kitted up to go out and he would change a driver or a commander and we would have to wake people up, just stupid pathetic power games. I was used to it but Molly wasn't and he was struggling big time with the bull shit.

243

Molly and I were on the lead wagon dropping of a few of the lads off to bolster the manpower at OP Tir. Nothing seemed right about it from the start, a mid-afternoon drop didn't make any sense as the place was getting hit three times a day from small arms fire. Minty was on the gun and commanding the rear Mastiff with Gwilliam as driver. I used to fume over this as driving the rear wagon was like a day off. The front Mastiff had a GMPG on it and the rear a 50 Cal.

As soon as the back doors opened to let the lads out, automatic gunfire exploded everywhere bouncing all over the wagon. Molly brought the GMPG on to the position and started ripping it apart. The OP Tir lads then started to fire from their Sanger and wall positions. Molly was screaming for Minty to open up on the firer with the 50 but nothing came. This was getting ridicules. An Observation Post called Dara then hit it with a javelin, wiping out the tree line. We done the exchange of lads and then went back to FOB Ouellette.

244

Zero was coming over the net saying a job well done and telling Molly he had killed 2 goats and it was coming out of his wages. What had happened was OP Dara had seen people in the treeline moving weapons all day and they needed a come on to get them into the open. An OP Archer is an operational feign to entice the enemy into reacting. OP Dara had a team on standby to wipe the insurgent point out when they opened up. They should have told us so we could have swapped Minty on the rear wagon.

I asked Gwilliam what had happened and he told me he tried to wrestle the 50 Cal off Minty but Minty was sort of frozen in position babbling. The Taliban have 7.62 ammunition so they are not really worried about GPMG, but when a 50 opens up they normally disappear. I laughed when Gwilliam explained what happened but Minty didn't want to talk about it.

27/07/2012 DAY ONE HUNDRED AND TWENTY SIX/ R AND R

I was finally leaving the CP to go on R and R. I had to drive myself down to FOB Ouelette in a Mastiff. I was the only one in the CP on R and R on these dates. I was glad to be going the CP was a mess, the ISTAR system had just fell apart and my head was wrecked. As it was a Friday the plan was to go to FOB Ouelette get a transport at night then dekit body armour and weapon then fly out of Bastion and arrive in the UK on Sunday.

I went to the gym had a shower and messed around on the phones and internet. I was imagining how I would spend my time on leave, who I would see and what I would get up too. I managed to get myself a decent bed space in the transit room, and kicked back reading when I heard a distant boom. I ventured into the welfare area. Everyone knew I was RTR and ran over to tell me what happened. A Mastiff had got hit on the 611 entering FOB Robb and the front wheel was blown off. It was the second wagon which didn't make any sense as the front choker normally gets it. A few hours later as I was preparing my kit to go the HLS Tucker and Mo come in stressed out. I give them some iced water and chatted for five minutes. The front wagon missed the pressure plate and they got it at the back. It was a small 15 kilo device enough to shake them all up and mobility kill the Mastiff. They were getting their heads down in the transit tent and then resigning for a new Mastiff in the morning. They were just sick to the back teeth of all the shit in the AO.

I bugged out and let them sleep. A few of us jumped into the helicopter which was a merlin. I was shattered and went to sleep. Bastion was a mess when we arrived and nobody knew were we were supposed to go. I couldn't stand the Welsh.

As soon as I woke up I knew something was wrong. The 1RWF ROG had arranged to brief us at 1400 which was far too late if we were supposed to be leaving at 1800. I handed my weapon and kit in and went to the gym. At 1400 there were around seven of us in a room with a 1RWF late entry Captain and a SM called Beefy. The LE Captain told us our flights were cancelled and that Tuesday would be the earliest for a flight, arriving in the UK on the Wednesday. He then asked for any questions, so I asked where any of the other flights delayed, "No", he then asked for any sensible questions, so I asked him were his R and R flights delayed for four days. He looked like he was going to explode and I was well prepared to go at it, but the SM Beefy, defused the situation by saying it was a fucking joke. I spoke to the LE and SM after and just told them I was sick of being messed around by their Regiment and anything they touched turned to shit, they had no answers.

My family at home were going mental as I was stuck in Bastion, I just went to the gym, sunbathed and went for coffee and meals. Bastion was a joke. On the queue on the Tuesday I ran into the 1RTR RSM who was flying back to the UK, so I flew with him. Things move a lot faster when you're with a RSM so the journey went quickly. He told me that the OP Beak lads had proved to be a disaster, most of them had blagged off the tour with imaginary injuries or shot themselves and the rest were always making excuses to spend time in Bastion. I knew it would be a mess. I met another G SQN Troop in Mynaid in Dubai. All of them had went on R and R as a oner and were coming back from the UK. It was good seeing them all, I wished I had been with this troop as they were based in a MOB and didn't do any STAG.

AUGUST

"One man with a gun can control 100 without one."

Vladimir Lenin

12/08/2012 DAY ONE HUNDERED AND FORTY
TWO/ AFGHANISTAN

I had been phoned by a 1RWF ROG Corporal to say
that I was going back to Theatre a day early that was
five days in total I had taken off my fourteen day R and
R. I screamed his fucking head off on the phone but he
was 1RWF and didn't care. When I arrived back in
Bastion instead of spending a few days there I was
transported straight to the HLS to return to CF Burma.

13/08/2012 DAY ONE HUNDRED AND FORTY
THREE/ BACK ON THE GROUND

I was 10 hours back in Afghanistan and I was in FOB
Ouellette, If only I had got back to the UK so quickly. I
went to the transit room and seen a 1RTR bed space, I
looked further and it was Molly's. Why the fuck was he
in Ouellette. I found him and asked him what was going
on, he was off the ground 2 months early. He said he
damaged his hearing, then he said he couldn't work with

McCullough, then he needed TRIM, then he couldn't

work with the Welsh. It was all balls he had had

enough. He said the CP was a nightmare and the

constant arguing was driving him insane. I wished I had

got off the ground early. He had been fighting with

Craig and arguing with Macca as well. On top of that he

had fell out with the 1RWF in the CP, as he couldn't sit

the tour out in OP Salat anymore he didn't want to

know.

When you arrive back from R and R you're supposed to

have 48 hours acclimatisation, I seen Mr Hoare in the

tank park and he asked me to go on the gun so one of

his lads could have scoff. I was back around 12 hours. I

told Suthers and Gwilliam to flip a coin, so one of the

drivers could go, this pissed the Welsh off big time,

welcome back. The lads who had flew in with me were

amazed I was driving as we had only arrived back, and a

few voiced their opinion to Mr Hoare, but it was fair

letting the lads get scoff.

I went back to CP Baray .I wasn't in great form. Everyone was slating Molly calling him a war dodger and a Jay Walker, I thought fair play to him get out of here. I requested a move to Pan Kalay to swap with Craig's driver Doyley who was struggling up there. I wanted to spend time with the rest of the troop, and it would have been class for a change of scenery. Mr McCullough just said no, but I couldn't understand why as I was a complete cunt in the CP. It was good catching up with the lads all the nonsense and war stories of 40 hour cordons. I told them about the RSM and meeting the G SQN lads the Boss was freaking out in case I had grassed him up for being shit, but I hadn't. I pretended the RSM wanted to see him as soon as we got back for a private discussion, and he kept asking why. I got my rounds back and bayonet and Sgt Dean give me a brief what was happening. He explained that we were handing the CP over to the ANCOP at some point and that they would be living with us for around a week. He was quick to say it wasn't his decision but I told him it was a fucking joke and he was going to get someone killed. He wasn't happy about it and said we would run angel STAGs, until we left.

ANGEL STAG

An Angel STAG is where an extra British soldier patrols the sleeping area of a CP in case of night attacks by ANSF. His rifle is made ready and he constantly monitors the ANSF, challenging anyone who wakes.

16/08/2012 DAY ONE HUNDRED AND FORTY SIX/ CO 2IC VISIT CP BARAY

Are OC and 2IC were in the AO today. Mr McCullough was flapping and kept briefing us to put a positive spin on things. I had no intention of doing any of this and was sick of hiding the problems in the Troop. Mr McCullough was hoping that when we got back the

255

euphoria of arriving home would colour things in a good light. Craig's multiple were picking them up and taking them to their CP, then they were coming to ours. The Boss didn't want us to wear black t-shirts instead he wanted us to look the same as the 1RWF lads so it looked as if we blended in. This was capitulation yet again to the Welsh as they were terrified we would tell the CO what they were up too. They knew he had the power to change things in the CP.

When he arrived he started to ask generic welfare questions, concerning people at home, use of sat phone, health, then he asked what are relationship was like with the 1RWF. I explained to him that the lads at Fusilier level were outstanding, that their SM was brilliant and that a few junior NCOs had a degree of professionalism. He got on to this straight away and asked me to explain what I had meant. I told him that it was a constant struggle dealing with their rank in FOB Ouellette, and that the CP hierarchy were a joke and treated us badly. I explained that certain people in rank buried there head in the sand and allowed the low level 1RTR lads too be abused. I explained to him the way the driver rotations worked, the constant doctoring of drivers hours, the way the entire CP was reliant on 3 drivers out of almost 50 lads. I explained to him that the gunners and commanders were not doing a full tour as they were always taken to OP Salat for a holiday ten days a month.

He said he would speak to the OC in FOB Ouellette and speak to Mr McCullough, weather he did or not I don't know. It was endemic in our troop to cover things up and put a gloss on everything. Weak soldiers call you a grass or a sniffer to hide how weak they are. If you do your job correctly you shouldn't be sacred of anyone.

22/08/2012 DAY ONE HUNDRED AND FIFTY TWO/ COMPLACNCEY VP 8

By this stage of the tour we were all counting days. Everyone was already at home and we had been setting patterns and fell into complacency on every patrol we carried out. Half the time we were driving past suspicious objects or hoax IEDs hoping either another patrol would ring them through, as we couldn't be bothered sitting in a cordon or cleaning weapons.

The Boss and Macca were out doing VP Checks at VP 8 and came under sniper fire. The cows in the fields knew were we were going to stop and knew the exact drill we were going to go into. Macca returned fire but couldn't PID the firing point so was firing blind, Mr McCullough didn't return fire as he hadn't a clue where it came from. When they got back to the CP there was gunshot mark on the side of Mr McCullough's Mastiff armour and a large hole you could put your thumb in. It was unusual and the first time I had seen a single round do so much damage. The truly frightening thing was it was around 20 inches downward from Mr McCullough's head in a straight line. The accuracy was intimidating and Mr McCullough was pure white. We all had a laugh at his expense. As it was a single shot and penetrated the armour we assumed that the round must have been from an old Lee Enfield bolt action rifle.

LEE ENFIELD (7.7MM)

The Lee Enfield bolt action, magazine fed repeating rifle was the main firearm used by the military forces of the British Empire during the first half of the 20th century. Many Afghan participants in the Soviet invasion of Afghanistan were armed with Lee Enfield's and they are still manufactured in the Khyber Pass region today. Bolt action rifles remain effective weapons in desert and mountainous environments where long range accuracy is more important than rate of fire. Despite the easy access to other more modern weapons the Lee Enfield remains very popular in Afghanistan.

25/08/2012 DAY ONE HUNDRED AND FIFTY FIVE/ BRIMSTONE 611

Macca and I were out in the rear wagon and Mr Hoare was on the front choker with Gwilliam. The rear wagon had no air con and it was a sweat box. We were out doing VPs and found an IED at VP 3. This was a nightmare scenario as it was a new Brimstone and they took ages. It was 0700 and we knew they wouldn't leave until they had scoffed and showered.

We blocked the North of the 611, and Mr Hoare took the South so it was easier to liaise with Brimstone. A pressure plate IED was buried by the culvert in shallow sand. The valon man picked it up and confirmed it. It was a Saturday, and that meant market day in Sangan. Brimstone and the OPS room in the FOB never went on the ground so they didn't understand the tension on the 611. All types of vehicles from the invention of the automobile stared to pile up at our roadblock. When the locals started to go mental or drive around us we just pointed the 50 at them.

Brimstone took hours to come out and we just sweating. Mr Hoare was informing zero that the road was building up and were encountering a lot of hostility. The OPS room in Ouellette hadn't a fucking clue and he was wasting his time. Generic answers were all they ever give.

Mr Hoare give Brimstone a full and comprehensive brief reiterating information six or seven times. He informed Brimstone not to deploy the IED bomb disposal robot as the sand was too soft and it would get embedded. For a reason only known to Brimstone they sent the robot down into the culvert and it immediately got stuck. Instead of reversing it back out and just blowing the IED up as a controlled explosion, they carried on until the robot wouldn't budge. Everyone on the cordon were furious, ignoring advice like this was a cornerstone of Brimstones MO they never listened. As they couldn't get it out, they had to order a crane from another AO as our crane was broke from hitting an IED. It was now 1500, and we had been there eight hours and we were now waiting on a crane from FOB Price and the heat was insane.

The locals started to slaughter their goats at the side of the road and throw the carcasses at us, women were holding their babies in the air screaming for water for their kids. The Taliban had destroyed market day and showed the locals and the Americans that yet again we couldn't provide security on the 611. Zero would not let us open the road and it was pointless engaging them. The crane from Price couldn't make it up the road due to the congestion and didn't arrive for four hours. When the crane arrived to lift the robot it took forever. To top it all off I got back into the CP at 2100 and was going to the gym and Suthers went sick for his 2200 patrol after sunbathing all day, meaning I had to go out again for another fucking six hour patrol.

SEPTEMBER

"When there is no enemy within, the enemies outside cannot hurt you."

Irish Proverb

01/09/2012 DAY ONE HUNDRED AND SIXTY
TWO/ ANCOP MOVE INTO CP

This was a nightmare. The ANCOP moved into the tents
in our CP today in preparation for the handover. The
ANCOP wanted everything they wanted the Mastiffs
the ISTAR and the communications system that was
used in the Ops room. We were giving them a fully
operational CP the best one in Sangan, equipped with 3
ten man tents, a solar shade, a working kitchen, hard
cover, two Sangers and they just wanted more. They
were completely fucking belligerent and always had
their hand out. Thefts rocketed in the CP and nobody
wanted to leave their bed space to go out on patrol.
Boots, socks, food were constantly being stolen. I went
out on patrol and came back and they had robbed my
MP3 and a lot of food from welfare boxes I had under
my cot bed. I hated them, we had BFPOs small radios
set around the camp which we were leaving any way
and they stole them.

265

The ANCOP are from the North of Afghanistan and speak a different dialect called Dari, were we only knew Pashto so it was impossible to relate to them. Minty couldn't find his gloves which are a mandatory item of PPE, there were a crowd of ANCOP standing smoking and the ANCOP commander was wearing Mntys gloves. The thieving scum just expected us not to say anything to him as he was the highest ranking ANCOP in the CP. Minty went and got his gloves back pulling them off his hands. I cocked my rifle and was well prepared to open up if it had have turned. The Commander was furious but I just stood looking at him with my rifle and Minty came back.

Mr McCullough then comes over and is disappointed with Minty and said he should have let him have the gloves. I couldn't believe this, everything was going missing and he was condoning there theft. It was a crazy decision which defied any semblance of logic for us to share a CP with these lowlifes. The ANCOP just sat staring at us, all day every day. Every minute they watched us. We kept a spotless CP, within 24 hours it looked like a rubbish dump. They destroyed the toilets by shitting on the walls and destroyed the showers by shitting in them. Every time we put rubbish in black bags, they ripped them open, emptying anything they didn't want on the ground. I thought the 3 Rifles were bad put these were a hundred times worse. We were unable to wash our clothes any more due to the risk of them going AWOL when we tried to dry them. It was a constant grind we had literally weeks left and we were put at unnecessary risk.

The 1RWF hierarchy in FOB Ouellette were that desperate to show progress that they kept putting lads at risk on the 611 by rushing handovers. Mr Hoare and Sgt Dean were so keen to look like golden boys they put their platoon at risk not only in OP Salat but now in CP Baray.

07/09/2012 DAY ONE HUNDRED AND SIXT

EIGHT/ ISTAR REMOVAL

ISTAR stands for Intelligence, Surveillance, Target Acquisition, and Reconnaissance, I just thought it was the camera system, up until we started taking the cameras down and it was explained. We started to dismantle the large camera system which protected our CP today. The ANCOP were going crazy and arguing with Sgt Dean and Mr Hoare demanding that they should be allowed to keep it. We were only a few days away from moving to FOB Ouellette, and I couldn't wait to leave. The ANCOP were becoming increasingly difficult and were at the point where their behaviour was threatening. They just refused to understand the reasons why we wouldn't let them keep the system.

The ANCOP soldiers followed their commander's behaviour and just snarled at us. We just carried on taking the system down. Across from the CP around

1km away a crowd of locals were watching the system come down. I informed Mr McCullough that half of them had phones and binoculars and just weren't the average local. He just shrugged. This was one of the hardest days we had and we could sense a change in the air.

ISTAR

ISTAR stands for Intelligence, Surveillance, Target Acquisition and Reconnaissance. In its macroscopic sense, ISTAR is a practice that links several battlefield functions together to assist a combat force in employing its sensors and managing the information they gather.

Information is collected on the battlefield through systematic observation by deployed soldiers and a variety of electronic sensors. Surveillance, Target Acquisition and Reconnaissance are methods of obtaining this information. The information is then passed to intelligence personnel for analysis, and then

269

to the commander and his staff for the formulation of battle plans. Intelligence is processed information that is relevant and contributes to an understanding of the ground, and of enemy dispositions and intents.

ISTAR is the process of integrating the intelligence process with surveillance, target acquisition and reconnaissance tasks in order to improve a commander's situational awareness and consequently their decision making. The inclusion of the "I" is important as it recognizes the importance of taking the information from all of the sensors and processing it into useful knowledge.

08/09/2012 DAY ONE HUNDERED AND SIXTY THREE/ MY BIRTHDAY BOOM

BOOM, 0600 leaving the CP. I was lead Mastiff with Mr McCullough commanding. I hit a massive IED under my wheel on the driver side. The choker missed the pressure plate and I hit it. The front of the Mastiff reared up like a bronco and fell back down. This vehicle was thirty tons. No words can fully describe the feeling of getting blown up. Parts of the wagon were found up to fifty meters away. The moment I was hit the windows filled with dirt and black smoke and what seemed like fire. I was thrown up in my seat with such force both seat belt straps snapped from the pressure. If I hadn't been wearing the belt my head would have hit the roof with such force my neck would have snapped. I had a policy of everything in the Mastiff being strapped down and nothing unnecessary being loose in the wagon. All passenger s were always strapped or I wouldn't move and all weapons were sealed in racks. The only items that I had loose were a water bottle, I placed my grab bag behind my seat.

Mason was straight up the back to see if I was okay, but I told him to go to Mr McCullough who had been standing up in the gunner's cupola. He was dazed and his face was covered in soot. He regained his composure quickly though and sent out a contact report. The lads in the back were all pure white. I didn't blame them, I was tone deaf and couldn't hear anything but a ringing which was like the sound in your ears after a rave. Suthers and Bob were in a Sanger and thought it was IDF and hit the ground the bang was that loud. This was insane, how did the insurgents get that close to the CP to plant a bomb effectively on our doorstep. The IED was placed 5 meters from the ANCOP Sanger were they had a 24hr permanent STAG and I believed they planted it.

Nothing made sense. The lads in the back of the wagon bugged out back into the CP and me and the Boss stayed with the wagon. The infantry pulled this stunt every time, just leave the tankies to deal with everything. Mr Hoare came down to see if we were okay and jumped in the back for a chat. The 2 Scots advance party where on QRF as they were taking over the AO from the Welsh. They came up in Warriors and told Mr McCullough and I to go back into the CP they would lift the wagon. You could tell they were new as they were that keen. They could not believe the sheer audacity of the insurgents to plant an IED basically in the CP. I was like it was probably the fucking ANCOP and of course Mr McCullough disagrees with me, when it was fucking obvious. I tried to wind Mr McCullough up using him as a Barmead, walking behind him across the ramp into the centre of the CP. He went off his head, but I kept doing it.

It would take around 3 hours to lift the wagon, so I went running and sorted some admin. I ran for 40 minutes then 20 minutes sprints. I had to go back to FOB Ouellette and sign for a new Mastiff, and do a tool check again. The REME were going to go crazy as we had only just attached the front Guard and choker a few days ago. Our rear Mastiff would follow on to the back of the 2 Scot Warriors in convoy.

Mason was telling me to relax and sit it out due to my hearing being shattered but McCullough wanted me to go, so there was nothing I could do. On the way down to FOB Ouellette Mr McCullough was telling me that he had been speaking to the ANCOP commander, and that they were grateful that we had hit it instead of them and it would improve the relationship in the CP. No shit Sherlock, the guy was incredible. When I got to the FOB Chris Lunn the REME full screw was just shaking his head, it was around 1100 and this was going to be an all dayer. The Driver always had to do everything,

1RTR gunners and commanders just walked away as soon as we went to the REME, and the infantry had a race to see who could get onto welfare first. The Boss went to the med centre and had a shower while I stripped another Mastiff for parts and assisted in rebuilding another one that they had in the FOB. All the REMFs in the FOB were getting photos by the IED wagon and I did as well. The only rank to ask if I was okay was SM Mills who told me that out of all the 1RTR lads in the AO I had had a hell of a tour and should be proud of the work I had done. I seen Mo, Jay and Reidey from the other 1RTR section and they were concerned for our lads welfare as it was pretty obvious that the ANCOP had planted it. I didn't even remember that it was my birthday.

09/09/2012 DAY ONE HUNDRED AND SIXTY FOUR/ ESCALATION

Tension was visible in the CP, we had gone from counting the days until departure, to freaking out about getting killed over breakfast. I just wanted to get home and my head was destroyed having to queue up behind the ANCOP to use the toilets. I heard an explosion to the North that shook the CP. It sounded like it was up at Pan Kalay and I was worried that our lads had been hit. I got ready and jumped into the front Mastiff, but we got stood down after around 30mins and placed on QRF, the PMAG had been driving past VP 9 and hit a fifty kilo IED which was buried under the road. Movement was cancelled across the AO until these lads were safe. At the side of the 611 at VP 9 runs a water system, which elevates the tarmacked 611. The insurgents dug into the side of the road and placed a command wire IED which they detonated bang on. The Mastiff fell into the water system, but no one was seriously hurt.

The Mastiff was brought to our CP that night for transportation to Bastion the next day as there was no space in FOB Ouellette. The damage was intimidating. This was another level of damage, if I thought my wagon was bad there's was ten times worse. The front of the wagon was missing, there were no engine bays. It looked as if someone had cut its nose off with a knife. 2 days two IEDs 2 mobility kills on wagons.

13/09/2012 DAY ONE HUNDRED AND SIXTY EIGHT/ MOVE TO FOB OUELLETTE

I was thrilled to be moving to the main FOB today. Improved gym, improved welfare, improved showers and improved scoff. The accommodation was far better. We got broken down into tents and I was made up I was with Gwilliam, Crochey and Coy. The only problem with living in the FOB was that it was the middle of the rip and the insurgents loved hitting it with IDF every few days. I seen the SM and he said that I was going to be busy during the rip. I told him I wouldn't be, that I would be expecting a 2 Scots driver to learn the AO the same way I did. He agreed with me and said he would tell Mr Hoare. You could avoid everyone in the FOB and I made full use of the gym every day.

The FOB was packed and the 2 Scots were coming in through Lashkar Gah. It was too dangerous for them to land in our AO. Some of the Welsh lads had got off the ground and Sgt Dean sent the 2 other drivers back to Bastion who had arrived in the AO after me. I spoke to Mr McCullough and said that this was just more pettiness and he should ask him what he was doing, but even at this late stage he was avoiding confrontation. 2 mortars were fired at the FOB but they only hit the perimeter wall so no one was injured. We also started handing in bits of kit that were spares to the Q department, it really felt as if we were going home.

MORTORS 82MM M37 AND THE 107MM M38

After the use of rockets, mortars are the most common form of indirect fire. The calibre used in an incident is rarely recorded. The 82mm M37 is easily transported

by man or pack animal and deployed to fire at large

area targets. Mortars larger than 82mm will be in

cantonments and caches however the ammunition is

used in IEDs. Mortars suffer from the same inherent

inaccuracy problems as rockets. Well trained an

experienced IDF teams are rare but are characterised

by a notable increase in accuracy. There is an endless

supply of 82mm in theatre.

14/09/2012 DAY ONE HUNDRED AND SIXTY
NINE/ IED ANA

I was in the gym doing speed work on a bike with a few
lads from the PMAG. An explosion sounded that
literally shook the whole gym. Everyone assumed the
IDF position on the ground, then sprinted to hard cover
in the welfare room. IDF normally makes a sound
before it explodes as it dissipates the air around it and
this didn't. But the closeness and vibrations said IDF. It

wasn't IDF, the information we got were that an IED had went off at OP Tir, they didn't know if it was an own goal, the lads at Tir, Americans or ANSF. That was my day ruined I knew I would be getting bugged out to sit all day at some cordon.

The inevitable shout came, Mac go and get your kit on and start the Mastiff, across a packed welfare room, everyone was made up that it wasn't them getting bugged out. My crew was Mr McCullough Bob and I. Bob was having issues with getting bullied but he wouldn't open up to me about it, I needed to get him on his own. The information we were getting fed was that a suicide based vehicle born IED had drove into an ANA base called CP Kakaer a few 100 meters away from OP Tir and detonated, casualties unknown. I honestly couldn't care about this as the ANA in CP Kakaer were always causing problems. When we got there the ANA were running around in circles, we managed to establish that 9 people were injured and 2 were killed. The scene in the CP looked like something out of a horror movie. There was a huge crater in the ground but no bits of car, it must have disintegrated on detonation. Bits of flesh were lying burned, scattered over the CP floor and the CP walls looked like someone had painted them in blood. We dropped off a team of medics and went to take our position up blocking the eastern access route.

We were contacted sporadically for around 2 hours but Bob couldn't PID the firing point so we didn't fire back, the Boss was asking him for directions and he was saying over there somewhere. All the other wagons were getting rounds off and we just looked stupid. MERTs flew in all day removing the wounded and bizarrely the 2 Scots QRF came down and relived us off our cordon after 4 hours. An average cordon was normally 20 hours, I couldn't believe it. On the way back to the FOB some clown in the Ops room decided that the Mastiffs could STAG on the gate at night from 2200 to 0600, which the RTR could manage, we were always getting gripped by them as well for driver's hours.

The night STAG was a joke and I readily informed Mr McCullough of this when we walked down to start it. He agreed with me as there were several security gates and a hill to enter the FOB. That's not what I meant though, the VBIED that hit CP Kakaer destroyed the place and was easily 80 to 100 kilos which would blow a Mastiff to bits.

CAMP BASTION

Camp Bastion got attacked today and two US Marines got killed. The RAF Regiment were caught sleeping and allowed a heavily armed Taliban Troop to slip through the perimeter wall. The raid was a complex and coordinated assault by 15 Taliban fighters dressed in US uniforms using several types of weapons which took place on the eastern side of Bastion near to the USMC aircraft hangars[1] at 22:00 local time (17:30 GMT). The assault team penetrated the perimeter of the camp and separated into three teams to carry out the attack. One team engaged a group of USMC mechanics from VMM-161 who were in the area, the same team had attacked the aircraft refuelling stations, one group attacked the aircraft, the last group was engaged at the base cryogenics compound. The group that attacked the aircraft attached explosive charges to several of the jets, then fired RPGs at several others. God knows what the RAF Regiment in the Sangers on the wall were doing but rumour has it that they were armed with pistols, as they were too lazy to go to the Armoury to sign out rifles.

15/09/2012 DAY ONE HUNDRED AND SEVENTY/ STAG CP KAKAER

I was with Macca and Bob in a cordon at CP Kakaer, it was driving me insane. Macca didn't have any cigarettes and was torturing Bob as he forgot to buy some. I didn't smoke so it was sending me crazy. Macca was telling Bob run across to another wagon and grab some. I was furious with this and was telling Bob not to go as we had been IEDed and took stacks of rounds in this village. Bob went and I knew he didn't want to go. This was breaking every drill in the AO. To send a junior rank on to the ground to get cigarette's from another wagon is criminal.

I argued with Macca over this but he was the commander. I had always got on with him and he had backed me a lot in the CP but this was fucking bullshit. Macca had kicked his crew off his wagon Des and Gwilliam, so there was only me and Bob left who would go on with him. Bob was letting Macca walk all over him and I was furious with this.

We argued over this all day and it carried back into the CP at night. I got off the wagon to do a last parade and clean the wagon but Mr McCullough came and got me and asked me to go to scoff with him. I explained that I hadn't sorted the wagon, but he told me to leave it, and asked Bob and I to come. Macca came into the scoff crew and started screaming at me for the state of the wagon, I told McCullough to sort it but he just froze. I went on the bounce and both of us where in each other's face. I was furious over this as I had never left a Mastiff without prepping it. I spoke to Mr McCullough over this but he was terrified, I explained that he had told me to leave the vehicle, then let me take the blame. I explained to him that as Troop Leader he had a duty to install discipline in the Troop and that his behaviour was boarding on cowardice. He just told me if I was going to do anything about it to leave him out of it.

16/09/2012 DAY ONE HUNDRED AND SEVENTY ONE/ 2 SCOTS RSM

Mr McCullough went out on a familiarisation patrol with the 2 Scots in the morning and left a few of us in the FOB. As soon as he drove out Macca started so I hit him a quick 3 punch combination to the jaw, and stepped in to uppercut but the only problem with this was Macca was 17 stone and I was just under 10 so he didn't flinch, we rolled about the ground of the Tank Park in the FOB beating lumps out of each other until some old Scots guy started screaming at us. Two lads pulled us apart and I was going to kick off as I didn't know who the fuck he was. On tour you wear what is called an UBEX top which has your cap badge and Brigade on it, no rank insignia. The two lads were standing either side of this Scottish guy were holding clipboards and shaking their heads.

The guy who was bollacking us was the 2 Scots RSM and he was going mental, he was telling us to report to the 1 RWF ops room. I spoke to him and explained that we only had a few days left of tour and we were just clearing the air as our Boss told us too. His face was pretty beat up and he looked like he was in a few scraps, so he was listening. The one thing Macca and I had going for us was that he was busy and busy people can't be assed if it's not their Regiment. We would have both been fucked if the Welsh had have found out about this and I believe they would have aimed for tour bonus. Macca and I agreed to leave it and not discuss it anymore and just laughed about. We had got on well for six months and it was pointless throwing it away for a bad day.

17/09/2012 DAY ONE HUNDRED AND SEVENTY TWO/ VIDEO FOOTAGE

I had a busy morning out training a 2 Scots Mastiff crew. I had a TA commander and a dangerously overweight gunner called Nelly, not because that was his name, because he was as big as an elephant. They refused point blank to listen to anything I said. The commander wouldn't wear his seat belt, helmet, eye protection or gloves and the gunner kept complaining he was tired. We were doing a complete run of VP checks and I explained that I was wearing my PPE because it worked in IED strikes and contacts, they weren't interested. The gunner hadn't loaded the 50 Cal and hadn't a fucking clue what he was doing, I had to jump up, load it and make ready, I was furious. I told them too just use one of their drivers next time as they knew everything and if I got dicked to go out with them again I would complain.

I was on a night patrol with the Boss taking Sgt Deans section out for no reason. Sgt Dean had been pulling this stunt for a few days, doing pointless patrols. He was asking his lads to take out cameras and head cams to catch footage for a tour video. Foot patrols that normally took an hour were taking up to three as he hung around known firing points, tonight he got his wish. Three firers opened up on the section with an assortment of small arms. Sgt Deans section opened up with bazookas, GPMGs, and hand grenades. The OPs room in Ouellette were kicking off all night asking what the holdup was, but everyone knew.

I spoke to Crouchey who was on the patrol, he was not happy. Crouchey had been shot in the abdomen on his last tour and almost died. He was the best soldier in the CP, and had one of the best attitudes of any of the welsh NCOs, he was 100% for the lads around him and hated seeing lads treated badly. He went and spoke to the SM and told him what was going on. The lads didn't go out again. Throughout the tour Crouchey always showed physical and moral courage, I wish I could say the same about some of our lads.

That night we got a brief. We got our dates for flying out and the Troops we would be moving into. 24/09/12 all of us in a few transports back to Bastion holiday camp.

24/09/12 DAY ONE HUNDRED AND SEVENTY
NINE/ OFF THE GROUND

Craig's section came down to the FOB with their kit. It
was the first time we were together as a Troop from we
left Bastion. The Pan Kalay lads had a busy tour and
seen some sites, but not one of them had been off a
vehicle and Craig had protected them and kept them
safe. The Gunners had taken the most risk in Pan Kalay,
as they always manned the Sangers in firefights whereas
there drivers went into hard cover.. They were much
more a section or a unit where the lads under
McCullough were a collection of individuals and were
deeply divided. We got a lot of photos taken, and talked
about what we were going to do when we got back. I
just went to the gym and played on welfare for the day.
When the time came to bug out it was 0230 in the
morning and two chinooks landed simultaneously. We
ran on with our kit and were off back to Bastion. When
we got back to Bastion the Welsh were as unhelpful as

they had always been. The hand in of bits of kit was done at 0530, and these guys didn't have a clue. Their rear Ops group in Bastion were the proper wasters of their regiment and they just screamed at lads. Forty per cent of their regiment had left in a year under the command of the people who were commanding us in theatre. Instead of cutting lads a break when they had just got off the ground we had to line up and hand kit back. I would be glad when we were away from these people.

CAMP BASTION 24/09/2012 – 26/09/2012

The facilities in Bastion were outstanding. I gymed it and sunbathed for a few days. I tried to avoid the Troop as the briefs were shocking. The Boss was briefing us not to complain or criticize anyone when we got back to our Regiment. Mr McCullough, Jay and Molly were pushing for the Troop to cover up the parts of the Tour where they didn't step up. My philosophy was it was their own fault that they took a back seat and allowed others to get fragged. Every single member of 11 Troop had an exceptional tour due to the amount of incidents. Too many people though sat back or dodged duties or hid in contacts through fear or idleness. Mo, Craig, Reidey and Biggsey had an amazing tour up in Pan Kalay, manning the wall in CP contacts and controlling fire on the wagons. In our CP it was very much the commanders and drivers who stepped up again as the gunners hid away. All I was hearing was that I would get promoted and I would get top Trooper. This was a desperate attempt to buy silence. There was simply no one close in the Regiment let alone 11 troop that had dealt with the amount of incidents that I did.

We handed kit back in and basically relaxed for a few days. Are contact with the rank was limited and I never attended any briefs. I seen the RSM and he was sound. All our lads on Herrick 16 were coming home in one piece at least physically. I asked him about the OP Beak lads and he said they were okay but falling over like skittles. We had decompression in Cyprus to look forward too, but I just wanted to go home and spend time with my family.

CYPRUS 27/09/2012

Cyprus was insane, the worst soldiers in 1RTR were running the decompression. I knew them all and they were a collection of war dodgers and biffs. In decompression you get a card which enables you to buy 5 cans of beer and that is your limit. As I rarely drink my mates Mo and Reidey asked if they could use my ticket. I didn't mind as I knew Reidey could handle his ale, and I was only going to give Mo two extra cans. 2 lads I was friends with were running the bar in Cyprus and give me around 20 cans. This proved disastrous because Mo got completely destroyed and was sick everywhere and pissed in his pants. He hounded me every few minutes to get him another can, and he was breaking the cans over his head. He had to be carried to his bed space and managed to throw up all over the accommodation.

HOME

"War has always been the grand sagacity of every spirit

which has grown too inward and too profound; its

curative power lies even in the wounds one receives."

Friedrich Nietzsche

RAF HONNINGTON 28/09/2012

We got back late as the RAF messed up our flight times. We were meant to arrive at 1400 and arrived at 1800 and they left our fucking kit in Cyprus, fucking Ryan Air. We had to go to RAF Honnington from Brize Norton which was 200 miles. I don't know why I couldn't go straight to Liverpool with the 1RWF as they were based in Chester. I was supposed to be going home, but Mr McCullough forced me to go. It took hours to get to RAF Honnington, for what was the weakest welcome home party in 1RTR history. A few cans of beer and some balloons and 2 or 3 peoples family. D SQN who were the RSOI SQN had bands and a carnival and they were based in the safety of Bastion.

I was literally there for 15 minutes then left to go to Liverpool. Captain Simmons the G SQN 2IC asked me why I hadn't went to Liverpool with the 1RWF as I lived there, I explained to him what had happened and he just shook his head. I drove home that night and got in really late the household was asleep.

I went back to RAF for an admin week to book ourselves into the UK. This is a joke however as only the single lads get punished or need adjustment as the lads who live on camp can go home to their families each night. Some of the 11 Troop lads were struggling emotionally and had mild cases of PTSD, (Post Traumatic Stress Disorder). This is very common in the first few months back as you transition from six months in a war zone to effectively normality. I spoke to a lot of lads and went for coffee with them. They were scared to report any mixed feelings to any rank or doctor due to the risk of losing or being restricted in your post operational leave. Some people take it badly and resort to alcohol, drugs or in some cases it can be expressed in domestic violence. The week wasn't too bad and I did loads of running and looked forward to having six weeks off post operational leave allowance.

Operational leave was outstanding. I went to the lakes and competed in a lot of road races. I spent a lot of time with my family and regretted going back to the Army.

Our Troop got split up on return and everyone just felt used and abused. I was glad however to be around new faces as some people were agitating me. We had a medals parade but as I was never down as serving in Afghanistan due to a clerical mishap I never received a medal. Every time I asked about it I was just ignored and that's when I decided to leave the Army. If the RHQ couldn't be bothered to pick up a phone or send an email concerning something as important as this, I no longer wanted to work with them.

I was asked by the G SQN OC Major Ford if I wanted to go to a cross party military parade in the Palace of Westminster. When we went it was exceptional and one of the best things I had done in the army. When we got there we were given complete access to the entire palace. We were told that anyone with a uniform could go anywhere unimpeded. When we went outside I met Nigel Farage from UKIP walking past and also the comedian Jo Brand, so it was an interesting day.

I left the Army on really good terms and got an honourable discharge, and I was proud to serve in the 1st Royal Tank Regiment.

AUTHORS NOTE

I was born in Battle in 1977 in Republican West Belfast,

Royal Victoria Hospital Falls Road. Civil war raged.

My Mum was in Labour when my Granddad was

getting buried, murdered by "enemies of Ireland". I

grew up in the militarised zone of Andersonstown,

FREE ANDYTOWN. I have fought IRA warlords,

Northern Ireland Drug gangs, the postcode gangs of

Liverpool in Prison, battled the fanatical Taliban, and

went head to head with the Crown Prosecution Service

several times. I have been kidnapped, interrogated, tortured, and stabbed with screwdrivers, Stanley knives, bottles, beat with hammers, baseball bats, Hurley sticks, attacked in segregation units, hit with plastic bullets, been shot at, mortared, blown up, hit with crowbars, beaten by gangs, and bitten in the face. I have been locked up in three countries and been approached by Special Branch to work for them, which I turned down, and been fitted up numerous times by the Merseyside Police. I have had false statements given against me by Halewood grasses and fitted up by a Prison Officer who was having a baby to a prisoner who attacked me. I have travelled the world, seen the Mona Lisa's smile, sat in silence in the Sistine chapel, stood in awe at David, viewed Van Goughs Daffodils, had coffee in Rembrandts house hunted for Machiavelli's grave, went up the lift in the south tower of the Twin Towers, climbed the Sydney bridge, had my passport stamped at check point Charlie and worked in a pub in Amsterdam's red light district.

This book is one chapter in my life there's more to come

The account is written from dairies and journals which I wrote in when I was over in Afghanistan. I have added reports from media outlets concerning events to add authenticity to the accounts from my journals. The details of the different weapon systems are taken from my training journals and notes from pre-deployment. I think it is essential information as people do not understand the threats that are faced daily in theatre. The photos were taken on an IPOD either by myself or by a gunner or commander from the turret of the Mastiff. I can be contacted on @mastiffafv.

I am currently working on a collection of short stories and a book detailing service in HMP Altcourse.